GOLD SHIMMER

IN THE SHADOWS - BOOK 4

P. T. MICHELLE

LIMITLESS INK PRESS

GOLD SHIMMER

IN THE SHADOWS - BOOK 4

In the Shadows Series
Reading Order

Note: Mister Black is the only novella. All the other books are novel length.

DEAR READERS: **GOLD SHIMMER** *is* the first book in the BLACK SHADOWS duet, Cass and Calder's happy-ever-after story. The duet falls within the main IN THE SHADOWS series. **STEEL RUSH** is the explosive conclusion to Cass and Calder's story. You don't have to read books 1-3 in the series to enjoy books 4-5.

To read Sebastian and Talia's equally epic love story, check out books 1-3, which must be read in the following order: **MISTER BLACK**, **SCARLETT RED**, and **BLACKEST RED**.

After you've read books 1-5, dive into book 6, **BLACK PLATINUM,** with an all new Sebastian and Talia stand alone, passionate adventure. Another Sebastian and Talia stand alone story, book 7, **REDDEST BLACK** follows, before you get to swing back to a Cass and Calder stand alone story with book 8, **BLOOD ROSE,** coming July 2018.

Happy reading! You've got lots of enjoyable books in the series ahead of you! :)

Look beyond the surface...

COPYRIGHT

SUMMARY

How far would you go to be with the man who stole your heart but doesn't know your real name?

GOLD SHIMMER is the first book in Cass and Calder's epic love story in the BLACK SHADOWS duet. STEEL RUSH is the explosive conclusion to their love story and it is now available. You do not have to read books 1-3 in the IN THE SHADOWS series to enjoy GOLD SHIMMER and STEEL RUSH.

I never thought that my plan to crash a masked party to exact a bit of revenge would fall apart so easily. Then again, I also didn't plan on running into a wall of sharp wit and steely determination named Calder while pretending to be someone else. The captivating Navy SEAL might've called me by Celeste's name, but he refused to let me hide my true self from him. His special brand of honest, seductive charm was impossible to resist. He was confident and demanding...and everything I wanted. But the deeper I fell, the higher the stakes rose while playing a role. So I held onto our intense connection for as long as I could, knowing that he would never know me as Cass.

When an unexpected turn of events gives me a second chance to see Calder again, I take it. Going undercover as Celeste once more, I'm plunged into a world of world of high-power wealth and privilege that's far more dangerous than I could've imagined. Everyone has an agenda, and lives are moved around like chess pieces. But for the one man who gave me the courage to live my life for me again, I'd do just about anything. Even become someone else.

DEAR READERS: **GOLD SHIMMER** is the first book in the **BLACK SHADOWS** duet, Cass and Calder's happy-ever-after story. The duet falls within the main IN THE SHADOWS series. **STEEL RUSH** is the explosive conclusion to Cass and Calder's story. If you want to read the other books in the series, Sebastian and Talia's happy-ever-after is contained within books 1-3 and must be read in the following order: **MISTER BLACK, SCARLETT RED** and **BLACKEST RED. BLACK PLATINUM** and REDDEST BLACK, all new stand alone Sebastian and Talia passionate adventure stories can be read after GOLD SHIMMER and STEEL RUSH. Then we get to swing back to Cass and Calder in a new stand alone story, **BLOOD ROSE**, coming in July 2018. Get started! You've got lots of enjoyable reading ahead of you! :)

IN THE SHADOWS SERIES:

WHEN I LEARNED JUST HOW UNFAIR LIFE COULD BE

CASS

The Past

I woke up on the porch swing behind Sherry's house, three hours past my curfew. My hands tremble as I quietly unlock our front door. I don't want to wake my parents. My dad flipped out when I was twenty minutes late last month. Shaking the wooziness from my head, I close the door with a soft click and use the handrail to pull myself upstairs.

The last thing I remember was talking to one of the football players about the game and seeing Jake Hemming chatting with another player across the room. Images keep flashing through my mind: Jake apologizing to me for acting like an ass last year. Jake looking adorable as he rakes his hand through his blond hair and invites me outside. The party noise at Sherry's fading in the background. He's smiling. *Flirting.* Did I dream that part while I was out?

Once I reach the bathroom and close the door behind me, I gulp in deep breaths. It feels as if my lungs are being squeezed and I can't get enough air. I run the tap in the sink and gulp down mouthfuls of water. My mouth is parched, like I downed a whole six pack, but I don't understand why. I only had a soda at the party.

As the shower pounds down on my shaking limbs, I rinse the shampoo from my hair and close my eyes, trying to recall the parts that I'm missing from tonight.

An image of Jake throwing his arm around my shoulders jars me. It feels too real. Then the memory rolls through my mind like a film.

He's leaning on me, apparently tipsy as he rambles about our football team's win against Saint Mary's. "I'm the only sophomore on the varsity team. I'm going places! Why can't Celeste see that I would worship her like a goddess?" he rails, raising his plastic cup in the cool night air, beer sloshing over the edge.

This is his way of apologizing? *I gulp down the rest of my soda so I don't say something snarky. "Maybe you two... just...aren't meant...to be." I shake my head and blink, confused as to why that had been so hard to say. It sounded clear as a bell in my mind.*

He grips my chin. "Ah, but we are, is that it, Cass?" he says in a husky voice.

Not any more. Not after what you did to me last year. *But no matter how shitty he treated me, my traitorous heart still skips several beats when his mouth moves close to mine. I guess I'll always want what I can't have. Stupid heart.*

Tilting my chin, he inspects my face. "You look so much like her it's freaky." When he throws his head back and laughs, I stare up at him in confusion. I know he's talking about Celeste, but...then nothing. My memory goes blank.

The steam in the shower making me cough pulls me back to the present. I'm shaking all over. *Why can't I remember?*

Squeezing my eyes shut, I press my face to the cool tile and force myself to take slow, deep breaths as I try to fill in the blank space.

Another image starts out blurry, then sharpens in my mind.

I'm kneeling in damp grass in front of Jake, his hand fisted in my hair, tugging hard. He yanks at his jeans' zipper, his words harsh, bitter. "I'm your god tonight. Open your mouth."

My eyes jerk open and I swallow the bile rising in my throat. It didn't happen. It *didn't* happen. Whimpering, I quickly swipe the fog off the shower door to seek out my jeans on the floor. They're dry, but mud and grass stain both knees. Covering my mouth with a shaking hand to keep the wail of humiliation inside, I shut the water off.

Why didn't I fight him? I question over and over as I pull on warm sweats and a T-shirt.

"Cass?" Sophie calls quietly when I try to tiptoe past her bedroom door.

I peek inside. "Hey, what are you doing awake so late?"

She raises a sparse eyebrow, a knowing look in her tired eyes. "Why are *you*?"

Despite my anxiety, relief rushes through me as I step in her room. My big sister will know what to do.

"You okay?" she asks as she beckons me over. "You know Mom and Dad will flip if they find out how late you got in."

With just a few wisps of dark hair sprouting from her bald head, she looks even weaker than she did yesterday. I want to be angry that she refused to go to her bone cancer treatment this week, but Sophie's been fighting it for two years now. I understand her wanting a break for just one day. The drugs that fight her cancer are slowly destroying other parts of her. *Fuck cancer!* I sigh and gingerly lay down on the covers beside her frail frame. "I'm fine. I just lost track of time while celebrating our win."

She *tsks* as she touches my damp hair, her brown eyes holding my gaze. "I smell mouthwash. Are you trying to cover the stink of liquor on your breath?"

Instead of reprimand, I hear nostalgia in her voice. At this moment I'd give anything for her to have fun at a party like other eighteen year olds instead of lying in bed, her body wasting away. The last thing I want to do is burden her with what happened to me. She'd get upset, and tonight she just doesn't look strong enough for that.

So I sigh and snuggle close. "Let's just say I learned my lesson. Why are you still awake?"

She flutters her hand down my cheek. "Can't sleep. Dad found yet another doctor to drag me off to, this one even more expensive than the last specialist."

I meet her gaze. "He'll never give up, Sophie. Not as long as there's *any* chance you can beat this. We *all* want that. Even five percent is five better than zero."

Clasping my hand, she folds our hands between us. "I know, but he needs to focus on building his business while it's growing, not finding new doctors for me."

I squeeze her hand. "You know Mom can't handle this kind of stuff."

"That's not what I mean—" She cuts herself off and sighs. "You know I don't want to die, right, Cass? You know I'd be here for you through thick and thin if I could."

I blink back sudden tears. Sophie has always been the ray of sunshine in our family. I used to tell her all my troubles because she always made me feel better. When she learned what Jake did last year, if she'd been stronger and able to go to school, she would've told him off in front of everyone. But she did give me good advice that helped me learn to cope and let it go.

Which I thought I had...until tonight.

Kissing her bone-thin hand, I give an encouraging smile. "You're going to be okay. Dad will make sure of it. And I will take care of Dad."

"You promise you'll help him stay on track, Cass?"

I nod and squeeze her hand. "Promise."

She closes her eyes and then opens them, her dark irises glistening in the moonlight. Releasing my hand, she touches my hair once more. "I miss having hair; I loved how dark and shiny it was. When I return, I'm going to come back as a raven."

I don't like it when she talks about dying, but I'm not surprised she's talking about reincarnation. She's always had a very enlightened viewpoint. It's her choice that surprises me. "Why a raven? Are you tired of being human?" I tease.

She shakes her head. "Ravens have strong constitutions. They can survive the harshest conditions and can eat just about anything. Not to mention, since I'll have wings, I can fly anywhere I want. I'll explore the world."

I frown. "Birds don't live as long as people."

"They don't die of cancer, that's for sure," she snorts out, then turns wistful. "Ravens can live up to forty years. That's plenty of time for me to see you go off to college, get married, and raise a family."

She's beaming. I haven't seen her smile like this in a long time, so I play along. "You planning on spying on me?"

"How else am I going to watch over you?"

Her sentiment makes my heart hurt. I cup her cheek. "You're going to do that anyway, big sister." Kissing her forehead, I slide out of her bed. "I'd better get some sleep. I have to help mom price out the stuff she's taking to the consignment store tomorrow. Who knew we could accumulate so much junk?"

"Good night, Cassandra. I love you."

"Love you too, Sophie. Now get some sleep and don't worry about Dad."

My conversation with Sophie bumps around in my mind as I pull my covers over me. But the second I close my eyes, more snippets of memory from tonight spark and flicker, bringing forth images I wish I could forget. Someone must've drugged my soda. That's why I didn't fight back... and why I passed out. As my heart races with anger and disgust, I bite my lip to keep my crying quiet. Swiping the tears away, I sniff back my worries and vow to tell Sophie what happened tomorrow. She'll help me get through this. She always does.

CHAPTER ONE

CASS

Six Years Later

"How about 'Claret' with a French pronunciation? You're the journalist, Talia. Be more imaginative with your fake name." I shut my car door as quietly as I can in the darkness, but it sounds like someone slammed a Dumpster closed, making my heart pound double time. A bird gives a low croak in one of the trees across the street. I instantly seek out the source of the sound. With a painful twist in my chest, I nod at the raven in the dim light and quickly kiss the inside of my wrist. *I wish I had told you that night, Sophie, but it helps to think you're still here watching over me.*

Coming around from her side of the car, Talia fiddles

with the red cape's tie around her neck. "Are you ever going to tell me why you do that?"

I shake my head, lips twitching. "Just remembering something."

She holds my gaze for a second like she wants to say more, then furrows her brow. "So names...what's wrong with 'Ella'? It's subdued and understated—"

"Do you really think 'Ella' goes with *that* outfit?" As we walk, I eye my roommate's sexy costume—a black leather corset over her peasant-style thigh-high dress, four-inch heeled boots, and a velvet-hooded cloak brushing against her fishnet covered legs—then shoot her a "give-me-a-break" look.

"Sarcastic much?" Talia mumbles and pats her newly dyed blonde hair around her carnival mask while we head up the long driveway leading to the Blake's Hamptons estate. Cutting her gaze my way, she slows a little. "Are you getting cold feet, Cass? Pretending to be Celeste to get us into this party was *your* idea."

Talia and I are as close as sisters, but we also have a code we've gone by ever since we became friends: Leave the past in the past. She has her baggage. I have mine. All that matters is that we're there for each other when the need arises. Attending this party is proof of that unspoken pact.

Tonight, we both get something we want.

"*Celeste* is our ticket in," I remind her. "The party invitation she posted on her wall, bragging about being invited, states attendees must wear a mask and use a fake name." Pointing to myself, I continue, "*Yvette* goes with my

French maid costume. Do you want me to pick your name?"

While Talia exhales and shakes her head, my insides continue to coil tight. Just saying Celeste's name does that to me. I'm proud of the fact that I no longer let my past rule me on a daily basis, but it sure as hell is riding me hard right now. It doesn't help that I spent most of today winding myself up about the event tonight, to the point I haven't eaten. Even now nausea is tumbling around in my rumbling stomach.

Everybody who's anybody will be at this exclusive party. Not that I care about any of that crap; it means there's a possibility Jake might be here too. I seriously doubt he's grown a conscience now that he's about to graduate college. The memory of Celeste's innocent expression back in ninth grade when she told me that Jake liked me rushes to the front of my mind. Like an idiot, I asked him if he'd like to go to the movies. His answer was to snort and loudly turn me down in front of the whole school. I can still hear his sarcastic tone grinding in my ears along with his laughter.

"You might look like Celeste, but you're nowhere near her level. It's bad enough she turned me down for Friday's dance, but I don't do middle class substitutes. Go back to being a nobody and stop trying to pretend to be someone you're obviously not."

There were at least three other instances throughout high school where I overheard Celeste turn Jake down. Her responses were different, but she always ended her rejection the same, "Too bad you ruined your chances with Cass." Of course that pissed him off, which inevitably stirred up a new round of gossip that lasted for weeks afterward. I could ignore that, but my anxiety that Jake might come after me, all because I looked like the girl who was too good for him, always spiked in the aftermath. It's like I couldn't get past it.

Damn Celeste Carver for shattering my naive belief that we're all created equal. And *fuck* Jake Hemming for ripping away my dignity. Celeste might not know everything Jake did to me after that embarrassing set up she engineered at school—as far as I know no one knows what happened during Shelley's party—but she never apologized for putting me directly in his path in the first place. It only took six years and loads of therapy for me to overcome the negative self-worth Celeste initiated and Jake fully inflicted upon me.

I might not be able to do anything about the past now, but I'm not above taking advantage of an opportunity to exact some payback either. Celeste cancelling her appearance at the party, then announcing she's going "social media free" for a weekend was just too perfect a scenario to pass up.

I just hope Jake skips this soirée. The thought of crossing paths with him makes me want to hurl. I swallow several times and fist my hands. The tension flexes the skin along my wrists, making the old scars itch under my French maid costume's fancy cuffs. *No more dwelling on Jake shit.* Resisting the overwhelming urge to rub my irritated skin, I grind my back teeth and tug the fitted sleeves down. Long sleeves were a requirement for my costume. Unlike mine, I'm pretty sure Celeste's skin is a blank slate.

"I'm sorry." I breathe out, hoping to calm myself. "I'm just a bit tense. I've never impersonated someone before." At least that's partially true. Knowing you can pass for your nemesis' twin versus actually pretending to *be* her are two entirely different things.

Talia nods, offering a sympathetic smile as we get closer to the door. "Vengeance against Celeste will be yours, but the last thing I want is to stand out at this party and alert Mina Blake's over-protective brothers to my presence. As soon as I get in there, I'm making a bee-line for the shut-away heiress and hope she's willing to share why she really quit college."

"You have major persuasive skills, I'll give you that, Talia, but I doubt Mina will just spill the beans about a potential drug ring on campus just because you bat your pretty green eyes and ask nicely. Why don't you at least appear to have fun for a bit first before you attempt to pump her for details for the school paper." I smirk and finger comb my dark hair around my own mask before adjusting the off-the-shoulder sleeves on my fitted silk blouse for maximum cleavage potential. "And bonus...if you give yourself a chance to relax, you might actually have a good time."

We step up to the door, and just as I start to ring the bell, Talia smooths the hood over the edge of her hair.

"Stop fidgeting with your hood," I say curtly. "There's no way they'll recognize you with that mask on. Even I think you went to extreme lengths dying your red hair blonde. A wig would've sufficed."

Talia immediately drops her hands and tucks them

under the cape's velvet folds, saying in a low voice, "I can't help it. If I get caught trying to see Mina again, I'm sure a restraining order will be in my near future."

I purse my lips and adjust the tiny fancy apron over the short, black silk skirt. "Maybe give up the idea of trying to talk to Mina tonight. That's one way to guarantee you won't get caught."

"I'm not the only one with an agenda, Miss Vixen-of-Vengeance," Talia says, her voice pitching slightly. "Care to call yours off?"

Making sure the choker around my neck is centered, I adjust my own black mask once more. Talia doesn't know the whole story. I told her about Celeste setting me up, but not what came later at Shelley's or the fact it dragged on. I just couldn't put the rest of the painful memories into words. I'd done enough rehashing in my own head to last a lifetime.

If Talia knew everything, she'd pass up her opportunity to interview Mina just so she could help me. But if there's even a remote possibility she'll also have a good time tonight, I want her to. She works entirely too much. My gut tells me her own past drives her to succeed, so I want her to take some time out for herself, just once. "Not a chance I'm giving up." Needing a distraction from dark thoughts about the past, I smirk and flick a foil wrapper in front of my roomie's face. "Just in case."

Talia's cheeks explode with color. "Put that away," she hisses, smacking my hand.

As I fold it under my fingers to ring the bell, I can't help but laugh at her muttered "Classy" comment.

While the chimes ring alongside the upbeat dance music playing inside, and Talia's distracted with her own nervous thoughts, I slip the condom into her cape's pocket. I do it partially in the hopes she'll discover it and finally get laid—I can't believe she's still a virgin at twenty-one—and partially to keep myself in line.

I learned a long time ago that sex can be as easy as breathing. It's like playing a game of pool or watching a movie. It's no big deal, so long as I control the *when,* with *whom,* and the *how.* Without protection, I'll only be able to get "Celeste" into so much trouble tonight. No wrapper, no body slapper. I have standards.

The real Celeste might deserve more for her part in humiliating me the way she did back then, but I didn't come here to completely smear her reputation. I'm not evil. I just want to rub away some of that gold, "better than the rest of you" veneer she projects to the world, and reveal her "common person" gritty metal underneath.

Talia and I arrived at the party forty minutes late on purpose. That way it would be in full swing and people would be less likely to pay attention to our entrance. As the butler pulls open the door, my best friend and I exchange knowing glances. He notices our well-chosen "costumes of lowly status," but doesn't skip a beat in inviting Celeste Carver and her friend inside.

CHAPTER TWO

THE OBSERVER

*A*ll the guests should have arrived by now. I open the car door, excitement thrumming through me.

Tonight I'm taking full advantage of this exclusive costume party's strict "mask and anonymity" rule. Maybe I'll frolic and play a little.

Through the darkness, two girls walking up the Blakes' driveway draw my attention. A blonde and a brunette.

I frown and close myself back in the car with a soft click. I don't recognize the blonde, but the brunette...surprise tightens my chest. At first anger flares, but then I calm down and mutter to myself, "Look who decided to show up after all. Tonight just got a *lot* more interesting."

With her face plastered on all the society pages, Celeste Carver is recognizable anywhere, even with her mask. It's the way she carries herself, that better-than-others stick up her ass, the arrogant tilt of her chin. The girl has the attitude down to a science. My gaze narrows. *Pretentious bitch. But no one knows her like I do.*

The girls disappear inside and the door closes behind them, muffling the party sounds. Before they showed up, I'd been content to just mingle.

When others don't know they're being watched, that's when their true selves rise to the surface. I could learn a lot that way.

But Celeste's presence changes everything.

I open the door and slip out, heading to the side of the house, my movements quiet and sure-footed.

I need to know what happens.

I must see her every move.

Study her. So I can *own* her.

CHAPTER THREE

CASS

The Blakes' gorgeous "beach" house, with its sweeping dual stairwells and opulent Italian villa style, is an open floor plan that spreads over to a bank of French doors, where a covered porch, a custom designed pool and private beach stretch beyond. The massive house highlights the wealth of one of the most prominent families in the country. My father's business didn't take off until I was in high school. Even now our family business isn't anywhere near this level, but we now have a house in the Hamptons ourselves.

I grin when the youngest Blake son, Damien, walks straight up to me. His black mask highlighting dark eyes full of wicked intent, he sweeps his short black cape back. Clicking his tall, shiny boots together, he reaches for my hand in an exaggerated formal bow.

Oh the doors Celeste's face so easily opens. I'm going to

enjoy making her have to knock before entering after tonight.

Spinning me around, the rapier at his trim waist swinging with his movements, Damien says, "Celeste, my love. You're going to be very distracting tonight."

"Ah, ah…" I wave my finger and drop my voice to bedroom husky. "It's Naughty Maid Yvette."

A confident smile crooks Damien's lips. "Ah yes, Yvette, then. I'm so very happy your plans changed. Would you allow this fox the first dance?"

I internally snicker at his affected Spanish accent, since the Spanish word for fox is zorro. This Blake definitely has a sharp wit. I bat my lashes. "Ah, Z, how can I deny a wily hero such a simple request?"

Gesturing toward Talia, I say, "I've brought a plus one. I figured you wouldn't mind. This is Scarlett."

As Damien smiles appreciatively at Talia, I notice Gavin's sudden focused interest in my friend before he starts across the room toward us. He's the one she's most worried will recognize her. My stomach tenses and I keep one eye on Talia while I flirt with Damien.

Then a very tall, broad-shouldered guy dressed in light brown buckskin pants and a matching shirt steps beside Talia just before Gavin reaches her. Clasping her hand, he lifts it to his lips and says, "I think the two 'hoods' should dance together for solidarity's sake. What do you say, Scarlett?"

Once Robin Hood pulls Talia away from Gavin and toward the dance floor, I allow myself to relax and take the glass of champagne Damien hands me. "Shall we dance?" he says as he tugs me the few steps down to the level where the crowd is dancing to an upbeat song.

As we weave through the crowd, a few people apparently recognize Celeste despite the mask and call out her name. One dark-haired guy dressed as Batman grasps my free hand, grinning widely. "Hey, Celeste! I'm glad you made it after all."

Just as I start to speak to him, a curvy blonde girl in a very revealing harem girl costume runs up, her boobs bouncing as she squeals in my ear. "Celeste!" Draping an arm around my neck in a vise hold, she spins me as she gestures to the crowd. "Look at this rocking party. So glad you made it."

"Yeah, uh...I couldn't stay away," I mumble, shaking off the champagne from my hand her fast movements had sloshed from my glass.

"Ooopsie...guess I've had a bit too much champagne," she whispers loudly in my ear, the smell of alcohol strong on her breath.

"Did you see Gavin, Jordan?" Damien says to the girl. "I think he was looking for you."

"Really?" Her eyes widen and she swivels around, looking for Gavin. "Where is he?"

While Damien untangles the girl's arm from my shoulder, then turns her in the direction of the bar, pointing out his brother, Batman guy says in a low voice, "Save me a dance later?"

"Sure," I say with a shrug just as Damien takes my hand

once more. Draining my glass, I set it on a side table, then wave to Batman as my host steers me into the mass of dancing people.

Damien has always been a flirt—I remember seeing him in action in high school, but tonight his hands have a mind of their own. While we engage in light banter about a party Celeste had supposedly attended last weekend but left before he got there, he slides his hands from my waist to my hips.

"So, *Yvette*...care to pick up where we left off..." he suggests in a low voice next to my ear, his fingers trailing lightly down my spine and across the top of my rear.

Tensing slightly, I paste on a smile and tilt my head, my grip on his shoulders tightening. "When was that exactly? I'm a little fuzzy on the details."

Damien barks out a laugh, sliding his hands back to my waist. "I don't know if I should be insulted or not." His voice lowers in smug confidence. "But if you need a reminder..." As he leans in close, his warm breath rushes against my neck with his kiss before his brown eyes meet mine. "I haven't forgotten the image of you standing in that greenhouse, water glistening on your skin after the misting system came on. If we hadn't been interrupted by Matt, I'd have made good on my promise to make you scream *my* name that night instead of his. Since Matt's out of the picture now, I have to believe the fates are shining on me. I've enjoyed each time our group has gone abroad and the obscene money we spent, but that weekend trip to Prague last year is one of my all time favorites."

A *weekend* trip to Prague? Private jets, estate homes, boatloads of money. I can't fathom living so extravagantly, even though I can picture what it must be like in my mind's eye. All that opulence on display. Maybe one day I'll capture a scene like that to add to my slowly growing portfolio. I took the photography class just to fill an elective requirement, but lately I've found it more interesting than my business classes.

"Fate has nothing to do with it." I breathe out a low, sultry laugh. "I'm sure all the build-up in your mind as to what could've happened between us would pale in comparison now."

"I'm willing to take that risk." While people dance all around us, he rubs a strand of my long hair that I'd curled in subdued waves instead of the big curls Celeste usually wears. "Are *you*?" he asks as he edges into my personal space to brush his lips against my cheek.

Before I get a chance to answer, someone taps him on the shoulder. "You're wanted over at the bar, Damien." The guy in a formal white military uniform jerks his chin toward the crowded bar. "Something about the beer taps being clogged."

Damien sighs and releases me. "Keep dancing. I'll be right back."

As he starts to walk away, I turn to follow. "I'll come with you..."

But uniform guy clasps my hand, saying in a low voice for my ears, "Stay and dance with me instead."

I barely give him a glance as I attempt to shake free of

his grasp. "I'm good." I don't want to lose sight of Damien. He's the biggest partier in the Blake family—not to mention the richest guy here—which means he'll be the center of attention. Celeste needs to be fully in the spotlight tonight when she does something beyond embarrassing.

The fingers around mine tighten, holding me in place. I frown and glance down at his hand on mine. "You can let go of me now."

"Why are you panting after Damien? Will only a slick billionaire meet your needs...instead of a lowly sailor?"

The arrogant challenge in his tone instantly stiffens my spine. I jerk my attention to his face, ready to lay into him for his assumptions, but I'm thrown off guard by his focused gaze staring at me.

As much as I want to study his defined cheekbones and angular jawline, it's his green eyes that hold my attention. Even shrouded by his hat's black bill, they're the clearest color I've ever seen. Lush, Ireland green. And currently full of judgment. Instead of taking the harshness in his tone too seriously—it's not like he isn't partially right about my agenda—my thoughts shift to how much I'd like to photograph him.

Shaking my head to get myself back on track, I scan the rest of his face. "You're not wearing a mask." As a matter of fact, he's the only one not following the "masks must remain on or you will be asked to leave" party rule.

He smirks. "Observant."

"Smartass," I retort, rolling my eyes. When his eyebrows shoot up as if surprised, I remember that cursing isn't

Celeste's style. She'll cut you down to size with her elitist attitude instead. Giving a half-smile, I tilt my head and gesture to his uniform. "Navy branch, right? Since you're not trying to hide, does that mean you're really in the military? Or are you just that incredibly arrogant?"

"And astute," he continues his assessment of me, his mouth crooking in amused appreciation as he runs his thumb along mine. "I'm in the Navy, and yes to your last question too." A shrug. "I can't be anything other than who I am, so why fake it."

His realness disarms me, while the warmth of his touch sets my nerves on edge, taking my stomach on a rollercoaster ride. I ignore the signs of interest blooming and instead focus on my inner "revenge vixen" who's currently rubbing her hands together in glee. He could be even better than Damien. Celeste would never spend more than a nanosecond socializing with a military guy. Then again, at least one of the Blakes must know him, because he's walking around unmasked. "Nice to meet you, Mr. Navy, I'm Yvette," I say, shaking his hand. "When do you ship out again?"

"Day after tomorrow." Turning, he leads me through the crowd. Once we reach the other side of the dance floor, he tugs me close as we begin to dance to the fast-paced song.

"Leaving so soon?" I say, letting disappointment creep into my tone.

His green gaze heats right before he clasps my waist and bends close to my ear. "I've developed a talent for getting to know people who interest me in record time."

"Really?" I raise an eyebrow as he straightens. "What's your secret?"

"I state my intentions right up front." He flashes an unrepentant grin. "Doing so cuts through the BS. Everyone wins."

The double meaning in his comment is hard to miss. This is probably the fastest come-on I've ever had. I love this guy's swagger. He's so damn cocky, he'll at least be fun to verbally spar with. The fact he's shipping out in two days and prefers to eliminate the BS in his life means he obviously isn't looking for more. I couldn't have planned a more perfect scenario. I'll get to have as much no-strings-attached fun with Mr. Navy-Hot-Pants as I want tonight, while at the same time stirring Celeste's snobby friends into a frenzy about her slumming it. I can already see their sidelong looks and hear the mumble of hushed gossip circulating around us. *Idiots.*

As unbidden excitement rushes through me, I laugh and tug free of his hold to grab two flutes of champagne from a passing server's tray. Turning back, I offer him a glass. "To an evening full of potential conquests...er, interests, Mr. Navy."

He shakes his head. "I'm staying sober tonight. And there's only *one* interest I'm focused on," he continues, moving closer to me as we dance to the song's rolling base.

Taking a long sip of my drink, I hold his steady gaze, ready to be enthralled by his methods. Or at the very least...entertained. "So, how *do* you employ this talent of yours?"

He rests his hands on my hips, the corners of his lips tilting in a predatory smile. "Blunt honesty."

At least he's consistent. "Honesty only gets you so far—" I gulp back a gasp when he pulls my hips fully against his. As he moves our locked bodies to the music's seductive beat, I'm shocked by his aggression, but even more surprised by his obvious erection pressing intimately against me. I quickly down the rest of my drink, letting out a low laugh. "Then there's the direct approach."

Determination shines in his green eyes flecked with bits of grey. "Damien's going to be pissed that I sent him on a fool's errand, but he'll just have to get over losing you. I'm not letting you go," he says in a low rumble, tracing his thumbs slowly down my hipbones.

I try to ignore the chill bumps quickly spreading across my skin from his arousing touch, but the resolute steel in his voice and tightening of his hands on my hips send a shiver of delight rushing through me anyway. I drain half the other glass, appreciating the warm buzz that's starting to spread through me. I'm well aware this seduction is all part of his "I must get laid before I ship out" plan for the evening, but for someone who's in total deception mode tonight, I appreciate the upfront honesty. "I didn't realize I was a prize to be won."

"Taken," he corrects quietly.

His husky double entendre rockets my heart rate. "You're pretty confident in yourself," I say evenly while my mind screams, *"Love it, damn it!"* Any other time I'd be all over this opportunity, but not tonight. Stepping back, I try to

slow the mutual attraction down to super sexy verbal fenc-
ing. "You...ah, do realize there are *two* pieces to this puzzle
you apparently want to complete."

Chuckling, he takes my glasses and gives them to
another server, then lowers his face close to mine. His hat's
bill briefly shrouding us in our own little shadowed space as
he slides his hands around my waist, amusement settling.
"Hmm, puzzle pieces...how is it that I'm just now noticing
you have so many intriguing angles, Celeste?" His serious
gaze drops to my lips, then slowly slides down my neck to
my cleavage before moving back to my face. Touching my
jawline, he captures my chin with his thumb. "I'm going to
enjoy fitting myself against every one of your curves until we
lock perfectly into place."

His seductive metaphor knocks me in the gut, wrecking
havoc on my senses. I'm really glad I gave that condom to
Talia or I'd get Celeste into so much freaking trouble
tonight. I can't decide if it's Mr. Navy's charmingly irre-
sistible confidence that's doing crazy things to my insides, or
his amazing smell.

He's not wearing cologne like half the guys here, but his
clean, crisp scent tightens my chest with an unbidden
craving for more each time he draws close, like some kind of
perfectly timed pheromone dispenser. My physical reaction
to his hold on me is so unnerving that I swallow, hoping to
settle the sensation. Just how far can he take this metaphor?
Nothing is hotter than a guy with sharp wit. "Let me guess.
You're a master puzzler?"

His lips lift in a definite smirk. "I'll admit you've

surprised me tonight, which doesn't happen often. I'm fasci-
nated. As for me being a master puzzler..." He pulls me even
closer. "Why don't you let me know once I've thoroughly
and completely solved you."

My lower muscles clench. *This man takes verbal fore-
play to a whole new level.* While my body zings to life, I
know his shrewdness doesn't bode well for my incognito
status. He obviously knows of Celeste, but he doesn't
really know her. That means I haven't been playing her
well enough, which could become a problem. She might
be a bitch, but at least she's whole. I look and sound fine
on the surface, but my insides are all broken. The last
thing I need is for him or anyone else to figure out I'm
not her.

Just as I push on his chest so I can rein myself in, I catch
quick movement out of the corner of my eye.

Talia is hurriedly weaving through the crowd. The way
she's pressing her lips together tells me something's up.
When I see she's also caught Gavin's attention and he starts
to quickly cut through the partiers, worry rises. I turn away,
mumbling, "I think Scarlett needs me."

I don't get more than two steps before Mr. Navy
captures my arm. His chest brushes against my back as he
says in a low tone, "Watch. This should be good."

The second Gavin steps into place, hot on Talia's trail,
the hooded guy who'd been dancing with her earlier grabs
Gavin's shoulder from behind. Despite the people all
around him, Gavin quickly jerks back, fist flying. The
hooded guy captures Gavin's swing as if it were a foam

bullet. Holding onto Gavin's fist, he says something in a low voice.

Mr. Navy's laugh rumbles in my ear. "If Bash's getting involved, then your friend Scarlett must've made quite the impression."

Whatever that Bash guy says works, because Gavin jerks free of Bash's hold, then tugs on his custom suit's lapels and walks away. All of this happens in seconds, so I scan to find Talia and keep my gaze focused on her until Bash catches up with her. When I see her nod and let him lead her out of the crowd, I exhale a sigh of relief. I know Gavin was her biggest worry tonight, and after that showdown with Bash, I doubt he'll focus on her again.

"Well, that was impressive," I say in a light tone. "Your friend has some skills."

"Yeah, he can hold his own. The guy grew up rough and doesn't take shit from anyone. He taught me a few fighting tricks even the military hasn't imparted. The streets are definitely a different kind of survival."

The last was said with amused affection and respect. I glance over my shoulder and meet his gaze. "You two sound close."

"Since we were teens. He always gives it to me straight, no lies, no bullshit. Other than my father, he's the only person I can say that about. Actually, he's the reason I joined the military." He smirks as he trails his fingers down a curl in my hair, stopping to wind the end around his finger. "Claimed it would be a more positive use of my skills."

It's on the tip of my tongue to ask what his skills are—

I'm dying to know—but then I notice the attentiveness in his touch and realize I'm acting entirely too interested and curious...more like me and *not* Celeste. This guy makes it too hard to pretend to be completely self-absorbed. Despite his poor taste in someone like Celeste, I don't like deceiving him. It feels wrong. I need to shift my focus back to Damien. He's much easier to keep up a superficial persona with.

I push my hair over my shoulder, swiping the curl from his finger. "What's your real name, Mr. Navy?"

His smile fades. For a second, I think he's not going to answer, but when he does his voice is tight. "Calder."

By his reaction, apparently Celeste knows him, and he assumed she knew but was playing coy. *Ugh*, I feel like shit for adding to his baggage, but sadly, not remembering meeting him in the past—because a sailor wouldn't rate high enough in her upper-tier social network—is exactly something Celeste would do.

I nod and force a smile to smother my guilt. "Thanks for the dance, Calder. Be safe when you ship out next week. I really should find Damien now. He's probably wondering what happened to me."

It's hard not to wince when I hear him mutter, "What the fuck..." as I walk away. But he really doesn't need the fucked up *real* me in his life either. I'm actually doing him a favor. Instead of turning back and apologizing, I walk through the frenzied crowd of dancers. While I scan for Damien's dark head and black cape near the bar, a loud crack of thunder rumbles outside, reflecting my suddenly tanked mood.

P. T. MICHELLE

Being a royal bitch *sucks*. I didn't think it was possible to dislike Celeste even more. At this moment, I despise her.

"Celeste!"

I'm knocked sideways just as I reach the edge of the dance floor as the blonde girl from earlier, Jordan, bumps shoulders with me, a wide grin on her face. My stomach drops at the familiar smell of a spicy cologne clinging to her. The scent elicits such a revolting response, I instantly take a step back

"Hey, girl," she slurs loudly to be heard over the music. "I ran into Jake a few minutes ago. He's looking for you." Glancing up, she nods toward the bar area. "Saw him up there getting a drink. And now I'm off to the bathroom."

My chest cinches when I follow her line of sight. Just then Jake's dirty blond head swivels toward us. Dressed as a gladiator, his eyes light up as they land on me. He must've heard her say his name. As Jake quickly speaks to his buddies, I try to grab onto Jordan's arm, but she's moving too fast and is swallowed in the crowd once more.

That moment I thought I could handle, the one where I face down the demon that I've slayed in my mind a million times before has come. As Jake heads toward the dance area, his blond head bent as he takes the first step down leading to the dance floor, my instinct is to run, but it's like my heels are welded to the floor. Everyone slows down around me, the sound fading to a heavy bass thump in the background.

What I wouldn't give to be smashed in the middle of the dancing partiers right now, hidden among their colorful costumes and gyrating bodies. I wouldn't even mind all their sweat.

Instead, I'm on the edge of the crowd, like a lone calf ready to be culled from the group. To be taken down. I swallow several times, hoping to at least bring the boisterous din in the room back. My ears only pop with a high-pitched sound. I've never felt more alone and vulnerable than I do at this moment. Well, except for the last time I talked to Jake Hemming.

CHAPTER FOUR

CALDER

*J*ust when I think there might be someone who doesn't give a fuck about the Blake family name, I'm proven wrong yet again. Only this time, instead of my connection to one of the richest families in the country giving me the upper hand, I'm *still* not good enough.

As I watch Celeste make her way across the dance floor, my brain stutters. Wait...so she knows that I'm in the Navy and doesn't bat a lash, but does she know I'm a Blake? I rack my brain trying to remember if I was introduced to her for the first time a couple years ago as a member of the family or just Calder. If she does know I'm a Blake, the sudden shift in her attitude just now makes even less sense.

I pull my hat off and rake my hand through my hair, then tug it back on my head, working my jaw in frustration. How screwed up am I that I'm actually thinking of telling her I *am* a Blake in the hopes she'll return to the interesting person she was less than a minute ago?

That's one thing I've *never* done—used my family name to get something I want. It's a move I'm vehemently against. Over the years I've learned to never mention my last name, especially when I first meet people. Yeah, I'm testing them, but I don't give a damn. I want any relationships I have— professional or personal—to be real and not because of my last name.

But tonight...Celeste was like two different people. Warm and interesting one minute, disconnected and cold the next. She's hot, no doubt; it's hard not to notice that about her. But I've never been attracted to her at such a base level before. Even now, I'm unable to keep my gaze from following her every movement. The way she moves as she looks around, her gorgeous neck and the curve of her shoulder begging to be kissed. *Bitten.* Fuck, I want to walk up behind her and sink my teeth into her soft flesh, to lock her to me until she realizes I'm the only one she should be focused on.

I'd blame my sudden attraction on alcohol, except I'm sober as hell. I really can't put my finger on why I couldn't stop staring at her the moment she walked in with that Scarlett girl. All I can think about is how good her soft curves felt against me, and how much I fucking loved the way she smelled, like an exotic summer breeze. Why is my brain ignoring the fact she stone-cold shut me down?

Because you want her, you sick bastard.

Where is it written that I need to like the girl I want to fuck?

Nowhere. The difference is...this one made me like her.

And then she ripped it away. It's like she did it on purpose.

Why?

I haven't wanted someone with such primal intensity since...

Ever.

I heard her breath hitch when my hand touched hers. I saw her gorgeous light brown eyes dilate when I tugged her against me on the dance floor. I've never had raw chemistry put me on edge before, and the fact it flared between us wasn't my goddamn imagination.

Fuck it!

Celeste Carver is a walking contradiction. She's not getting off that easy. Setting my jaw, I start across the room.

CHAPTER FIVE

CASS

*S*omeone steps up behind me, his voice a low, angry grate in my ear. "If you're going to tell me to fuck off, I want you to say it to my face." The sound of Calder's deep voice ramps my pulse, but his icy words twist the knots tighter in my stomach. "I want the truth, Celeste."

When a guy stops Jake to say something to him, I'm finally able to tear my gaze away. Exhaling my relief, I turn to Calder, my voice a desperate rasp. "Dance with me."

He captures my wrists in a tense hold, his jaw turning to stone as he scans my face. "Don't play games with me."

I swallow and quickly shake my head. "I'm not."

Pressing his thumbs against my pulse through my cuffs, the anger in his expression thaws and his brow furrows. "What is it?"

Calder's suddenly alert stance reflects natural, protective instincts. My heart twists, making me wish we'd met under different circumstances. Just as I hear Jake's voice call out, "Hey, Celeste," I tug free of Calder's hold and push him back into the crush of partiers on the dance floor. "What are you waiting for?" I say, my voice pitching higher as I force a light tone.

A slow song starts up, and the crowd pairs off around us. Instead of wrapping his arms around me, Calder captures my jaw to keep me from avoiding his gaze. He stares into my eyes, his own full of questions. *What the hell is going on? You're not telling me something. What was that earlier on the dance floor? Why did you walk away?*

I wrap my arms around his neck and press against his hard frame, trying to keep the trembling inside me from surfacing. "I'm sorry I was shitty to you. I have no excuse."

When he lowers his hands to my waist, tensing against me, I'm surprised by how much the thought that he might push me away yanks at my heart. I tighten my hold on him. "That's the truth, Calder. I promise."

Calder reaches up and pulls one of my hands down from his neck. Holding the back of my hand against his chest, he massages my palm, his steady gaze searching mine. "Tell me that the attraction is real, Celeste. Tell me that I didn't fucking imagine it."

Hearing Celeste's name, I close my eyes. I'm falling deeper into this web of lies, but I don't know how to get out of it. Not right now. And with Calder's arm surrounding me as we slowly turn on the dance floor, his warm fingers sliding along my palm, God help me, but I don't want to. In this moment, I envy Celeste's life. She doesn't have a Jake haunting her past. Even better, she has Calder right here in her present.

"Tell me the truth."

The deep baritone in his voice goes all the way to my knees. I force my eyes open and meet his gaze. I can't lie to him. I don't know why, because I constantly lie to guys; I've lied to every person I've been with. But with him staring at me so intensely, I just can't. "You didn't imagine it, Calder," I breathe out.

He hooks his finger on my chin, his green gaze mesmerizing me. "Why does my name sound like a moan whenever you say it? That's all I hear, and it's so damn arousing."

Every word out of his mouth is freaking provocative. I inhale slowly to keep my breathing even and answer lightly, "Wishful thoughts perhaps?"

Dipping his head, he rasps in my ear, "Not wishes, these are very much carnal *intentions*. I want to hear you saying my name over and over, to feel your desperate need while you beg me to let you come. I'm going to soak up every syllable, every glorious, breathy gasp as you fly apart."

Panic seizes my chest, but I rein it in and pull back, smirking. All I need to do is diffuse the situation and direct his thoughts elsewhere. "You're incredibly confident." My sarcasm has a sharper edge than I intend, but it's enough to stiffen his shoulders and narrow his gaze.

He stops dancing and folds his arms at the base of my spine. "Are you challenging me?"

I shrug and slide my arm around his neck once more.

"Lots of guys think they're great in the sack, but it turns out...most aren't."

A dark scowl creases his forehead, his hold tightening around me. "How many are we talking about?"

"Do girls count too?"

As surprise scrolls across his face, I push up on my toes and squeeze his neck lightly, whispering in his ear, "If you expect numbers from me, you'll have to share yours too. Why do I have a feeling ours will be vastly different?"

He grunts and locks me to him as he begins to dance once more. "You won't find any *men* on my list."

Despite my nerves winding me up, making me feel like I'm about to snap, I snicker and let Calder move us to the slow beat. I'm determined not to look back toward Jake. I don't want a reminder that he's in the same room. I want to pretend he's not here. To go back to the confident girl who walked into this party. To be Celeste.

But when I allow myself to fully relax against Calder, his hard, muscular frame molding to my soft curves as we sway to the sensual music, I only want to be Cass with him.

I'm thankful Calder seems content to dance and not drill me with questions. I don't want to have to explain my change of heart to him. And really, it's not like it was a change. As Calder tucks my smaller body fully against his tall bulk, the pressure and warmth of his hands heating my skin through the thin silky material of my costume's fitted top makes my insides tingle. I rest my head against his shoulder and settle into a dancing rhythm with him that feels right, despite tonight's craziness. In the circle of his strong arms, I feel protected, like nothing and no one can intrude on this perfect moment.

I lift my head when Damien suddenly appears and taps Calder on the shoulder, his gaze drilling into him. "Turns out there wasn't a problem with the beer taps, but I had to handle something anyway, so thanks for keeping Celeste company. I'll take over now."

Calder's shoulders tense under my arms and he shakes his head. "Sorry, Damien. She's staying right where she is."

Damien's mouth tenses and his mask-framed gaze narrows on Calder. "Are you trying to make sure you don't get invited to the next party?"

"I really don't give a damn." Calder shrugs, his tone blasé. "I might see you in a year or two. Might not."

While my heart jerks at his flippant reference to his upcoming deployment, Damien visibly stiffens. "What the hell is it with you two always causing trouble?"

Two? Ah, he must be referring to Bash, considering his earlier confrontation with Gavin. I put my hand on Damien's arm to diffuse some of his anger. "I'm sorry, Damien. I really don't think I would've lived up to your expectations anyway." *He has no idea how true that statement is.*

Before I can pull away, Damien captures my hand and turns it over to kiss my palm. Raising his dark eyes to mine, he says, "I have a feeling you'll fulfill many. We can pick up where we left off..." He pauses and cuts a smirk Calder's way. "Once he runs off to save the world."

Calder's hands cinch on my waist. "Walk away, Damien, before you can't."

I'm surprised when Damien just laughs at his curt tone, then slides his gaze to me. "Don't feel sorry for him, Celeste. He's too damn stubborn to get killed."

Shaking my head once Damien walks off, I mutter, "I can't figure guys out. At least girls react normally to each other when they're pissed—bitchy with claws bared."

Calder's bark of laughter is cut off by a loud rumble of thunder rolling through the room. It shudders the walls as if perfectly timed to introduce the house music starting up. When the music level jacks even higher, the crowd goes wild around us, people raising their arms and jumping to the crazy beat. While the gathering storm amps their excitement further, they cheer even more when a loud clap reverberates and lightning illuminates black clouds in the sky outside.

I hold on tighter to Calder so I don't get knocked over and laugh at the people acting like nuts. At the same time the power flickers, sending the group into further frenzy, my gaze locks with Jake's dark eyes. He's watching me from the edge of the crowd, lust, jealousy, and sheer want evident in his gaze.

I swallow and force myself not to look away, cringe, or shudder at his steady regard. I'm not Cass. I'm *Celeste* who has always given him the brush off. Taking a page from Celeste's book, I keep my expression impassive. Once I slowly slide my attention back to my dance partner, the sight of Calder watching me so intently sets my heart racing.

We're suddenly jostled when a guy spinning a girl

around bumps us. The second they hit, she squeals and her champagne sloshes across my hand on Calder's shoulder.

"Shit! I'm sorry, man." The reaper guy turns, eyeing Calder's wet jacket.

"You need to apologize to her," Calder says tersely, glancing at me.

"It's fine." I quickly wave the guy and girl off, then try to swipe the dampness from his uniform. "We should get a towel to soak this up so it doesn't stain."

Clasping my hand, Calder tugs me off the dance floor, past the mass of people at the bar.

When we pass through a swinging kitchen door, a couple of fairies are standing on opposite ends of the massive island, giggling drunkenly. Hands aloft, golden crystals trickling from their clenched fists, the girls freeze in the middle of their glitter sugar fight and turn guilty looks our way.

"It's time to leave, ladies," Calder says in a commanding tone as he removes his hat and sets it on the corner of the island.

Instead of focusing on the girls, my attention briefly snags on Calder, specifically the two sharp points of ink on his skin just above his collar. *What is his tattoo?*

The girl with curly blonde hair closest to us let's out an annoyed grunt, drawing my gaze back to them.

"Fine, be a killjoy." Once her friend with a black pixie cut comes around the island to stand by her side, they exchange devilish looks, then toss their handfuls of glittery sugar toward us like wedding rice, giggling uncontrollably.

"What the hell..." Calder snaps as the golden cloud scatters all around us, but we all pause when the kitchen lights go out and the music suddenly stops. Someone yells through the silence about the DJ having a generator, and the second the music starts pumping once more, the girls squeal their excitement and head back to the party through the swinging door.

Grunting his annoyance, Calder walks over to the door and turns a latch at the top, then glances my way. "At least they won't be able to return with reinforcements."

I'm thankful for the dim light coming from the flashes of lightning outside. I can still see him without being tempted to stare at him. My stomach dropped when he first tugged his hat off and I saw his whole face and light brown hair. The man's sinfully good-looking. With enough champagne in me to be dangerous, I panic. My skin feels all warm and tingly now that we're alone. Needing a distraction from my thoughts, I start opening drawers in the island. Grabbing a hand towel from the second drawer, I wave him over. "See what happens to killjoys," I say lightly, snickering while I attempt to wipe away the glitter stuck to the splatter pattern on his shoulder.

Calder grimaces as he taps the bill of his hat on the island's charcoal gray marble surface to shake off the glitter. "At least I wore an old hat tonight."

Scanning my gaze over the gold glinting in the darkness across his light brown hair, I sweep the cloth over his other shoulder, keeping my movements brisk while brushing the loose glitter away. "It looks good on you. Kind of gives you an ethereal glow."

Calder captures my wrist and pulls the cloth from my fingers. "Trust me, there's nothing otherworldly about me."

My heart races when he lifts my hand to his lips and presses a warm kiss to my palm.

"I'm just a man; all flesh and blood," he says in a low rasp before moving his lips along my hand. Kissing my fingertips, he murmurs, "This is what real feels like," and then wraps his lips fully around my index finger.

I exhale sharply at the hot warmth of his mouth and tongue sliding from the base of my finger all the way to the tip. The pleased rumble in his throat as he licks the glitter off and rasps, "I knew you'd be an interesting mixture of sugar and spice," tightens my belly and lower muscles. This isn't a good idea. My emotions are all over the place with this guy.

I try to tug free, but his hold on my wrist just tightens, his warm fingers folding around me. "You smell so good, all I can think about is tasting every part of you," he says before sucking on the heel of my palm. His action sends electric pulses shooting through me; I'm immobilized by the heat of his mouth and arousing words. Tensing, I know I need to move out of his hold, but before I get a chance to pull away, he puts his other hand on the countertop behind me, blocking me in.

"You're going to give us a chance," he says gruffly as he folds my hand across his neck.

"I am?" My attempt to muster sarcasm fails. I just sound breathless instead. *Damn this man.*

He grips my waist and leans close, his masculine smell enveloping me, stealing my ability to think. "I made the mistake of letting you walk away from me earlier," he says while inhaling along my throat. Following the same path with his mouth, his searing heat jacks my heart rate even higher. "I won't let you go this time."

"Let me?" I chuckle at his dominant arrogance even as my fingers tighten on his neck, pulling him closer. "It's called free will, Navy. You don't own me."

A low laugh rumbles from his chest, vibrating against mine as he slides his lips along my jawline. "When I'm done with you, the only place you'll want to be is in *my* bed the rest of the night. You will most definitely be owned."

I press my other hand to his chest, enjoying the feel of his hard muscles under his uniform. "You're pretty sure of yourself. And just how do you plan to do that?"

He kisses my nose and then licks the corner of my lips. It takes everything inside me not to respond to his seductive worshiping of my face, but I manage to remain still as he presses a tender kiss in the same intimate spot before he lifts his head and meets my gaze.

Running the pad of his thumb along my bottom lip, he follows the path with a hungry gaze. "I can't wait to taste your mouth."

"What's stopping you?" I ask, my chest tightening. I want to feel his mouth on mine. To know if he kisses as aggressively as he talks.

He shakes his head slowly, his gaze never leaving my lips. "I won't until I hear you begging me to let you come."

My eyebrow hikes. "And how do you plan to do that? Molten stare me into a frenzied state?"

The corner of his mouth lifts in amusement for a split second before his heated gaze snaps to mine. "I'm going to devour your pussy first. You won't be able to hold anything back while you're writhing and begging me to let you come. I want *all* of you. And when I'm done lapping up all the pleasure I've given ..." He leans closer, and just when I think he's going to kiss me anyway, he clamps his teeth on my bottom lip with enough bite to flood my core with throbbing want. Sliding free, he holds my gaze. "*Then* I'll taste your sassy mouth, Celeste."

"Don't call me that," I snap before I stop myself. I'm shaking inside by the things he makes me feel. All the feelings he evokes—want, desire, arousal—only make me more anxious. Not only am I *not* the person he thinks I am, I'm the biggest fraud on the planet. I talk a big game, but I'm sexually dead inside. No matter how hard he tries, he won't be able to get me there. And knowing this makes me feel physically ill, because...this man...I *want* him to.

Talia might technically still be a virgin, but at least her battery-operated-boyfriend can make her come. Even though I tease her about getting laid, she has no clue that I've never climaxed. Apparently I'm the best actress to every man I've been with. None of them know that I faked every orgasm. Every. Single. One.

Calder's chuckle pulls me out of my worried thoughts.

Lifting my hand, he presses his lips against the cuff on the inside of my wrist, his voice low, intense. "If you want to be someone else tonight...Yvette doesn't suit you."

Be someone else. As soon as he says it, the answer comes to me...the perfect name. Hearing *that* name won't make me tense. She's brave...far braver than I've ever been. She would've been there for me if she had known. I think about the raven I had inked on the inside of my wrist a couple years ago. It stands proudly on the gorgeous tree branch the tattoo artist expertly drew over the scars, incorporating them into the bark. Calder can't see the tattoo hidden under my cuff, but it's like he subconsciously knows where to point me with just a simple statement.

Tonight, I'll be her. A girl full of sunshine. A girl afraid of nothing. Not even death.

I fold my fingers around his and meet his gaze. "Call me Raven."

A pleased smile flashes. "Ah, a name that implies cunning and shadowy stealth to go with your intriguing sex appeal. I fully approve. Raven is perfect." Releasing my wrist, he skims his gaze over my hair as he runs his thumb along the edge of my black mask. "The gold shimmers in your dark hair like your eyes do when you're amused."

His comment makes my stomach flutter, but I shake my head. "Brown eyes are so bland."

"Not yours. They shine." Leaning close, he rests his left hand on my shoulder, then slides his thumb along the front of my throat and under my choker, commanding in my ear, "Put your hands on my waist and hold still while I take care of something I've should've done the moment you walked into the party."

"What if I don't want to stay still?" Despite my question, I lower my hands to his hips and try to ignore the chill bumps rising on my skin as he runs his nose down my throat.

"I might hurt you," he husks right before warm lips sear the skin just above my choker.

"Intentionally?" I whisper, my fingers gripping his white jacket as his other hand slides down my ass.

Warm breath bathes the curve of my shoulder, and at the same time his thumb dips into the hollow of my throat, he releases a pleased groan. "You smell so fucking good, I could devour every bit of you."

I gasp when he sinks his teeth into the soft spot between my shoulder and my neck. It's so unexpected, so purely primal, my sex floods with heat. As my knees wobble, my instinct is to flee. Not out of fear, but because I'm so incredibly turned on. I want to know just how far he'll go, how raw he can get. Clamping his teeth on my shoulder is an act of dominance, not meant to break skin, but applied with careful and measured force. He's marking his territory, laying a claim. On me. No...on Celeste. The tantalizing sensation of his body against mine, his tight hold on me, makes it hard to remember that I'm not the woman he wants. He makes me want to forget who I am completely and let him have free rein.

While my brain fights every instinct for me to lean into him, he grips my ass tight and kisses the side of my throat once more, the pressure of his lips bone-meltingly intimate.

Thunder rumbles and lightning flares in time to the rising bass of the rave music in the other room. The ramping sound goes straight to my rapidly beating heart and vaults my pulse even higher.

With every short breath I take, his amazing smell draws me in deeper. I remind myself this won't end well. I'm guaranteed to disappoint Calder. In so many ways.

As I slide my hands to his chest, intending to push him back, he captures my chin and nips my jawline near my ear lightly, his voice a low, mesmerizing hum against my heated skin. "No flying away, Raven mine. I'm nowhere near done claiming every part of you."

My heart jerks when he clasps my waist and lifts me up onto the counter. Eyes wide, I stutter, "Wait, you're going to...here?"

"Where better to savor you than in the kitchen?"

I bite my lip, excitement racing through me at the idea of him going down on me in a near public setting. Reaching up, I run my finger along the two dark points of ink peeking a quarter inch above his jacket's stand up collar.

"This could be anything: the point of a star...a letter. Some say that tattoos are scars worn on the outside. I think of them as the most intimate part of a person."

"Most intimate part?" He folds his fingers around my forearm, unknowingly touching my other tattoo underneath my shirt's sleeve. Pulling me closer, his hooded gaze darkens with sexual hunger. "I'll show you mine, if you show me yours."

I exhale a slow breath, my lips twitching. "Do you really

think I have one?" I deftly avoid confirming his assumption as I pull free to reach for the first gilt gold button.

He captures my wrist, stopping me from unbuttoning his collar. "I'd lay money on it."

I arch an eyebrow. "You're not going to let me see yours?"

"You'll see all of me soon enough." A grin, full of sensual promises, flickers. Stepping between my legs, he rests his warm hands on my thighs, skin to skin. "For now I want to hear you beg me for it."

He's so freaking arrogant. "Good luck with that." I pick up his hat and set it on my head, then salute him. It's sad how honest that statement is, but I might as well enjoy the build up.

"Smartass," he mutters, tugging on the bill to bring my face close to his.

His mouth is a breath away from mine as he flattens his palms along the marble on either side of my hips. His nearness fills the air with an electric charge that runs all the way to my toes. How did the fun banter shift to something much more intense so quickly? I need to keep this light, a bit of raunchy fun. "Strategizing, Mr. Navy?"

A dark smile crooks. "Always," he says right before he clasps the insides of my thighs. "Lay back."

I gasp at the cold transferred from the marble to his hands, but the chill on my skin only ramps the heat between us. Exhaling a calming breath, I lower myself down to the cool marble surface. I need some space from his heady magnetism. But my anticipation only ratchets higher as he slowly slides me on the slick, glitter-covered surface until the back of my knees hit the island's edge.

As he grasps my thighs, his gaze slides leisurely over me. Lust flickers in their depths and his firm grip loosens. "I'm discovering a whole new appreciation for glitter."

I bite my lip while he begins to rub the golden flecks from his palms along the insides of my thighs, his movements methodic and sensual. When he reaches my short skirt and flips it out of the way, the thin red ribbons holding my silky black underwear together at each hipbone draw his attention. Pausing, his gaze flicks to mine, full of carnal heat. "This just keeps getting better and better."

"Only if you use that cocky mouth of yours for more than just talking." Exhaling a sigh, I raise my arms above my head and stretch, undulating my hips in a move that I know drives guys crazy. "Do your best to solve me, Mr. Navy. That is...if you're up to the challenge."

His lips twist as he leans over me. "There's something you should know about a good strategist."

"And what is that?" I say, my words coming out in a breathy whoosh when he plants a kiss on my belly button.

He lifts his hooded gaze my way. "We study every angle, learn every possible move that can be made for the very best outcome, and then we implement a solution."

I slide my fingers in his hair and gold flecks shower down on my belly. Trailing my fingers along his hairline, I halt at his temple. "And what's your success rate?"

He grips my hips in a firm hold and runs the flat of his tongue along my stomach. Licking up every bit of glitter sugar, he rumbles against my suddenly prickled skin, "One-hundred-percent."

His attentiveness makes me so wet, I almost hate that I'm going to ruin his record. Even though he'll never know he didn't succeed, I feel it's only fair to warn him. "I'm not so easy to solve."

He slides his hands to my ass and chuckles as he nips at my hipbone. "Complicated, are you?"

When I mumble, "I'm a double-sided, 3D puzzle," he glances up at me once more, his gaze suddenly serious.

"Every puzzle has a solution, Raven. I'm yours."

Before I can rib him about his overconfidence, he lifts my right thigh and kisses a searing path toward my sex, rendering my brain useless.

The closer he gets, the hotter my body radiates against the cool marble. Chill bumps layer over flushed skin. The combination is so stimulating, I rock my hips, encouraging him as I let out a breathy sigh. "I'm enjoying your strategic moves."

Biting lightly on my inner thigh, he shifts to my left leg, lifting it up to press a kiss along the inside of my knee. As he trails his tongue in a swirling pattern down my leg, his warm breath bathes my skin while he slowly makes his way to the edge of my underwear.

I'm surprised when he turns and presses his nose against my sex. Inhaling deeply, he groans. "You're soaked and fucking hell you smell like dessert."

His teeth nip the edge of my underwear, and I jump, gasping.

Just when I start to reach for the ties holding my panties together, he grunts and glares at me. *Stay still.*

I sigh and move my hand to his hair, heart hammering while he slides his teeth along my underwear until he reaches the bow. Clamping his lips around the end of the ribbon, he pulls it free of its loop, then does the same to the other side.

I bite my lip as he dips his head and presses a soft kiss to one side of my sex and then the other. When he continues pressing his mouth tenderly along my sensitive lips—just light pecks, not full on contact—I furrow my brow in confusion. *This is his idea of great oral?* I'm thinking he exaggerated that one-hundred-percent satisfaction rate.

I dig my fingers into his scalp and hope he gets the hint, but he only moves lower to plant a chaste kiss right against my damp opening.

What the hell? My whole body is tightening, waiting for him to proceed. "What—what are you doing?" I say as I start to sit up.

He flattens his hand on my belly, his action entirely dominant while he patiently answers against my body, "I'm getting to know you."

I point to my head. "My brain is up here. You can get to know it later."

He glances up and smirks. "This part of you has a brain too, angel. Trust me."

"Angel?" I snort. "At the moment, the devil on my shoulder disagrees. This," I tug lightly on his hair, " is pure physiology. No thinking going on."

He pulls my hand from his hair and places it on my belly before he moves to drop a kiss on the bit of dark hair covering my mound. His movements unhurried, he murmurs against the hair, "This is perfect. Just enough."

"Just enough for wha—"

I arch off the counter and swallow a shocked gasp when he bites down on my mound with enough force to instantly wake every nerve ending in my body. I throb everywhere with intense, jaw-grinding want.

Releasing me, he holds my widened gaze. "Are you ready for me to fuck you now?"

His voice might be calm, but hunger swirls in his eyes. Reeling from his shocking primal move, I barely get out "just taste me" before he dips his head and slides his tongue inside me, taking our flirtation to a deeper, more intimate level.

As he alternates between stroking me with his tongue and sucking my clit, my stomach tenses and moisture floods my sex. I wind my fingers in his hair, tugging him closer and vaguely think that I can never pull him close enough. What he's doing feels *that* amazing.

"You taste so good," he rasps, angling my hips to allow him deeper access. "So fucking addictive." As I try to catch my breath, he takes full advantage of the position, plundering me with his tongue and jacking my heart rate higher. Sucking and nipping at every inch of my sensitive skin, he makes me feel like he's worshiping my body.

Calder's style is unlike any man I've ever been with. His extremes throw me completely. He's intimately possessive, his mouth coaxing my body along like he knows me better than I know myself. Unbidden gasps and moans escape as I move my hips with his rhythm while he takes me so high that a fine sheen of sweat coats my skin. At this rate my ass is going to have a layer of gold it'll take a loofa in the shower to get off.

As the tautness builds inside me, my elevating heart rate stutters. I know I'm about the reach the point of no return—that awful place where my body completely shuts down—I tug hard on his hair, desperate to suspend this fantastic ride. Usually now is when I'm screaming and bucking and getting louder, letting the guy believe that he's the best I've ever been with. But the pleasure Calder's giving me is indescribably body-consuming; a nerve tingling, fan-fucking-tastic high.

No one has ever gotten me this far. But despite my wishes, the dark wave is coming. I already feel its murky cold water spilling over the edges of my euphoria as it crashes against the dam of my mind, demanding to be set free. It will smother this amazing physical build-up and flatten every single response.

It always does.

So I start moaning deeper and breathing harder. I rock my hips and press desperately against Calder, grabbing his head. *Faking the hell out of it.* "Calder...I'm...going to—"

He jerks upright and my thighs lower to the counter. His expression is intense as he leans over me slightly to cup my sex. "Don't speak. Just move."

"What?" I pause my movements even as panic flushes my face with heat.

"You heard me. Not a sound. Not yet."

"Why?" Exhaling to cover the sudden shakiness in my voice, I gesture to the door. "They're not going to hear me over that music."

Holding my gaze with an intense one, he slowly dips a finger inside me. My body instantly reacts and I arch into his hand. I swallow a genuine moan when he adds another finger. "I want to feel you come. No distractions. Understand?"

But louder breathing, exaggerated hip rolls, and bucking...they're all part of my perfectly choreographed repertoire. *I'm the best comer ever. And now he's trying to take that away from me? Hell no.* I shake my head. "I don't think I can be silent."

His expression intensifies and he thrusts his fingers as far as they'll go, possessing me deep inside. "Do you want to come?"

I don't like him honing in on the most broken part of me. Like he's mocking me. Sarcasm surfaces when I feel cornered. "You wouldn't be between my legs if I didn't."

Folding the heel of his palm around my mound, he tugs and I zip down the slick counter toward him until his face is just over mine. "Then stop faking it."

CHAPTER SIX

CASS

I gape and blink as shock rolls through me. "I'm *not*."

"*Yes* the fuck you are," he says, his hold tightening.

How the hell can he tell?

Running his thumb along the sensitive spot where my leg meets by body, his tense expression settles. "Just relax. Let it happen."

"Easier said than done," I say truthfully. "I'm on a countertop, laying here like a party smorgasbord with people just outside the door." Let him think I'm having stage fright. The alternative is much worse. *Oh yeah, did I forget to mention I'm unsolvable. You'll be trying to find that missing puzzle piece all night and end up with lockjaw.*

"I have plans for us after." He glances toward another door that leads off the kitchen. "But if you'd like a room now..." Before I can object, he takes his hat off my head and then scoops me in his arms.

With my mask suddenly pressed against Calder's warm neck and his amazing smell doing indescribable things to my insides, true panic sets in. It's one thing to mess around with him while people are just a door away. It's another thing entirely to steal away to a quiet space where he'll expect me to get naked.

I *can't* be alone with him. I'm not Celeste. She doesn't have a single tattoo. I'd know if she did, because she would have posted it on social media the day she got it. *How did I let this get out of control so fast?* As he takes a couple steps, I cup the side of his face and press a kiss to his jawline. "Here is fine, Calder. I'll try to relax."

His serious gaze scans my face. "Are you sure?"

When I nod, a pleased smile flickers. Kissing my forehead, he murmurs, "That's my girl," and turns back toward the island.

His girl. Damn that just makes my heart ache. I'm insane, but I can only blame it on his intoxicating scent. The musk of want radiates off him, drawing me in, making me want to spend more time with him. The man runs so much deeper than I could've imagined. He shifts from cold to hot, from simple kisses to extreme passion in a blink, yet his complexity absolutely fascinates me. I don't know what to think of him...other than I could bury my nose in his warm neck and inhale all night long.

Calder lays me down on the island once more, and even though he's standing to my right, he puts his hand on my stomach when I try to sit up. "Lay still," he commands, his hand already moving to clasp my inner thigh.

While he runs his left hand along my shoulder, then up my neck to my jawline, his right hand inches higher up my thigh. The music thrums at a frenetic pace, but his movement toward my throbbing sex is excruciatingly slow. His gaze has never left mine and I clench my inner muscles, pulsating with the need to feel his hands and mouth on me once more, his fingers possessing me even deeper than his tongue.

"Calder—"

"Not a word." He quickly bends close, his mouth a breath away from mine.

I smell myself mixed with his masculine scent and before I think better of it, I slide my tongue along the seam of his lips. I need to know what we taste like together. When I run my tongue along my own lips, a low, feral growl erupts from his throat. Our combined taste is salty sweet with just the right amount of passion mixed in, and the flavor only makes my stomach clench more. Just as I start to press my lips to his, he clasps a handful of my hair and holds me still.

Breathing in and out in harsh gusts, he releases my hair and jerks my legs toward him. Swiftly lifting my right leg over his shoulder, his mouth connects with my sex in voracious need, like we've been lovers for years and there's no build-up necessary, nothing but mutual want and pleasure. I moan, enjoying his rough aggression only to be even more turned on when he anchors my other leg to the counter, opening me fully for his greedy mouth. His groan of approval vibrating against my body shakes me deeply.

"Fuck, I can't get enough," he rasps, then plunges his tongue deep along my center, devouring me like a man who's gone too long without a meal that truly satisfies.

My heart jacks and my hips move on their own, seeking release to the build up, shocking the hell out of me. I have never made it this far. I'm gasping for air, my stomach tensing, my thighs trembling.

"Cald...so good. I can't even—"

"No sounds," he commands.

I gulp back the wail clawing to let loose from my throat and arch my spine, pressing wantonly against his talented mouth.

But when he latches onto my clit and sucks it hard, my quiet huffs vault to excited, erratic pants.

Tension curls in my belly, pleasure drawing from every pulse point and centering on my core. The sheer bliss of the moment threatens to turn my heavy breathing into full out screams of pleasure.

If I call out, he'll stop and that's the last thing I want. I'm climbing, climbing so high the darkness feels far, far away. I don't want to fall down into that black abyss.

Grabbing his hat by the bill, I turn it so I can inhale his intoxicating scent while these amazing feelings are spreading through my veins in a fast moving, prickly heat.

As I rock my hips, I know the hat won't muffle the shocked wail of pleasure rushing up my throat, so I clamp my lips on the rim.

When my body starts to shake and my inner walls begin to convulse, I swallow my shock as it registers that an orgasm is taking over my body. *Holy shit!* Biting down on the leather band, I hold back the cry of release that bursts past my lips. It feels so good to let go and allow myself the freedom to experience the ultimate pleasure that has eluded me for years. And I gave it all over to a complete stranger. At the moment, I don't care how fucked up that makes me.

"That's it, angel. Give it to me. Every last delicious drop," Calder grunts against me, his voice suddenly gruff.

Just as I press shamelessly against him, he pauses briefly and murmurs, "All for me," before he presses a hot kiss on the sensitive spot where my leg meets my body. While I revel in the feel of his mouth in a place I never thought of as erogenous, he slowly lowers my other leg to the countertop. I pant as his warm breath rushes against my wet sex. He flicks my clit with his tongue before he begins to roll the bit of skin between his tongue and lip. When he pinches the sensitive bud, then tugs on it, teasing my body mercilessly, he finally does what he promised. He delves his tongue impossibly deep, fucking me, possessing me...taking me to another plane.

He's so aggressive, I'm nudged across the counter, but he yanks me back and burrows as close as he can get, his teeth and mouth taking me to a new edge of pleasure and pain. His actions are primal and raw, giving me the most authentic, intimate moments I've ever had with another person. I move higher, euphoria keeping me just outside the edge of embarrassment at the sound of him lapping up the heavy rush of desire dripping down my sex.

When Calder pauses and glances up at me with insatiable lust in his gaze, I take several deep breaths, unable to form words, let alone believe that I might just come once more. And even if I can't get there right away, I wish I had the freedom to try all night long. I wish I could say the words he wants to hear: *Take me to bed. I never want to leave it.* They would be completely true. But that is the last thing I'll be able to say tonight.

With a confident smirk, Calder dips his head toward my body once more. Just as he connects, a closed door on the far side of the kitchen opens. I quickly push on his shoulders, then jump down at the same time I grab my underwear off the counter.

Two guys stand in the doorway their gazes locked on us. One is dressed as a prohibition era gangster, while the short, thin one blinks behind a full jester mask and hood. The gangster guy smirks, then says something about getting a bag of ice before they both quickly proceed to the fridge and pull open the freezer.

My fingers curl tight around my underwear and I feel my face flaming, despite the mask. Reality bursting our bubble of intimacy forces my brain to reengage. Of course it's just my luck to stumble across the one man who managed to make my body sing while I'm pretending to be the person I despise most. Worry quickly rises to the surface, fast and furious. How will he react when he finds out the truth?

He'd been adamant about how he feels about being lied to earlier. I should've kept my distance and stayed away. I just didn't think things would progress this far. I didn't think he would give me a mind-blowing orgasm.

I didn't think at all.

I assumed he'd be easy to walk away from, like all the guys before him.

God, I was so wrong.

Calder tugs his hat back on his head, his expression impassive. From my position beside him, I see the fast rise and fall of his chest. He's just as affected. Correction...he'd been caught up in *Celeste*.

While the two guys lift the huge fifty pound bag of ice out of the freezer drawer, I swipe my free hand across the counter, then blow the gold sugar dust off my palm. As the sparkling dust settles I say in a low voice, "Don't be distracted by gold's shimmer, Calder. Underneath the shiny polish, it's just a lump of metal like any other."

He frowns and starts to say something when the bag of ice drops on the freezer door, knocking it off its hinges. "Can you help, man!" one of the guys yells to Calder as the bag splits and ice begins to spill out.

Once Calder quickly rushes over to help with the rupturing plastic bag, I turn and leave through the doorway the guys came through, ducking into a small bathroom. Thankfully the power is still out, so no one can see how flushed I feel after I come out of the bathroom with my underwear now intact. Unfortunately the darkness also hinders my ability to locate Talia. I step down into the dancing crowd, trying to blend in while I look for her. I really hope she got what she came for, because I need to get out of here, *now*.

My stomach swirls with nausea and worry sets in when I can't find her after I walk a circle around the dance floor. I must look like I need it, because a passing server offers me a glass of champagne. I take the drink and down it in seconds, then instantly regret it. My head is buzzing and my stomach feels even less settled.

Setting the glass on a table, I turn, intending to resume my search for Talia when I run right into the guy dressed as Batman.

"Celeste!" he says, smiling as he clasps my shoulders. "Dance with me?"

Well, shit...I'd promised I would. I nod and pull him into the crowd, hoping I'll catch a glimpse of Talia out here on the dance floor somewhere.

"I can't believe we've never done this before," he says casually over the music.

I stop scanning the room for my roommate and focus my attention on him. The muscles he's wearing are all costume. On the slim side, he's around five-eleven with dark brown hair and a nice enough smile. I have no idea who he is, but apparently Celeste must by the way he's talking to her. "What? Dance?" I ask, curious how they know each other.

He nods. "Yeah...well, party actually. It's kind of funny considering we're close in age."

I shrug and give a half smile. "Different circles."

A frown furrows his brow briefly, but then he laughs. "I

guess so. It's not like I've gone to Europe with you and your entourage."

What the heck does that mean? I don't get a chance to ask, because I suddenly see Calder on the edge of the crowd, sweeping the dance floor with a serious gaze. The look of frustration on his face sends guilt shooting through me. Even as I move so Batman blocks me, I feel awful about ditching Calder. *I suck.* Regardless, he's going to be pissed at me, but at least this way, he won't hate me completely. Right now he's annoyed, but if he finds out I lied to him about who I am, he'll be royally pissed. *Where the hell is Talia?* I wish I could text her, but one downside of my skimpy costume is there aren't any pockets for a phone.

I take a chance and peek around Batman's bobbing shoulders as he moves to the fast paced song. My heart jerks when I don't see Calder. *Where did he go?*

Then I see his white hat and broad shoulders weaving through the crowd, his expression determined as he surveys the dancing people all around him.

"I—I suddenly don't feel so well," I say to Batman.

When I start to turn away, Batman clasps my shoulder, then points to my right. "The bathroom is in that direction, along that wall."

"Thanks."

As I dart away, he calls over the music, "Talk to you later, Celeste."

I wince that his voice seems to carry, but quickly duck around half-drunk partiers as I head in the direction of the bathroom and away from Calder.

I glance back to see if Calder has spotted me, and when I note that he hasn't I exhale to calm my racing heart. I turn to face forward and run right into Jake.

"Whoa, hey!" he says, grinning as he clasps my arms. "I've been looking for you all night, Celeste."

Heat flashes as fear and rage swirls through every nerve ending in my body. Hearing him say Celeste's name brings the past raging back.

I'm on my knees, wet grass soaking my jeans. I feel weight on my shoulder and my hands are held behind me. What the hell? Heavy breathing gusts against my neck. Someone is holding me in place.

Jake tilts my chin up, his gaze glittering with power and smugness. "I'm going to be your god tonight, Celeste. Open your mouth."

My mind isn't my own, because I gasp as I stare up at him.

He tsks, then tugs down on my chin as he strokes his erection. "A bit more, sexy."

Moving his hand to my head, he yanks at my hair. "Kiss me like you've always wanted to. This is the only kind of kiss I'll allow you."

I start to shake my head, but he tugs me forward and presses the hard tip of his cock against my lips.

My jaw flexes and he groans as he slides his cock inside my mouth.

Looking down at me, he commands, "Suck me off. Worship my dick."

His fist tightens in my hair and he moves me up and

down his erection. "Ah, that's it, Celeste. Fuck yes, take me deep." Lust sparks in his eyes as he stares down at me, his hips jerking. Twisting his hand in my hair, he yanks me forward.

The guy behind me—one of Jake's teammates?—was chuckling at first, but now he's pressing against my back, his breathing heavy along my neck. "Fuck this is hot," he murmurs as he slides his hand between my legs and cups my crotch through my thin skinny jeans. "Come on, babe. Enjoy this," he grates in my ear as he begins to run his hand back and forth, rubbing me.

My mind feels disconnected from what's happening to me, but my body reacts despite my wishes. I shouldn't feel any kind of pleasure. This isn't what I want!

The guy laughs against my neck. "I feel how wet you are. You gonna come for me, baby? May as well get something out of this too..."

The smell of alcohol on Jake's breath and his signature cologne brings me back to the present, and a swift gag reflex rushes forth. As fear and rage swell within me, I swallow back the bitter taste. He's smiling and flexing his fingers around my arms.

You're Celeste, not Cass. You're Celeste. I feel my chest rising and falling and try to get a grip. *He doesn't know you're Cass. Be Celeste.*

"Hey Jake." I shrug free of his hold. "I've got to go."

When I start to walk past him, my head held high, he laughs and pulls me against his muscular chest. "Come on, dance with me, Celeste."

71

The moment I tense in his arms, the confident cockiness in his smile fades and a flash of vulnerability reflects in his gaze before shifting back to friendly appraisal. "You ready to graduate? How long has it been...two years since we last saw each other?" He reaches up and touches the edge of my mask, his voice softening. "Damn, you're even more beautiful."

Nothing drills home the fact that he doesn't realize I'm Cass faster than his deferential treatment of Celeste. He's being sweet and attentive, practically begging her for attention. That combined with the feel of his sweaty body pressed against mine explodes the simmering volcano inside me.

I shove against his chest. "Don't touch me," I hiss out through gritted teeth as he stumbles back.

Jake blinks at me in surprise, his hands held up. "What'd I do?" When he tries to take a step toward me, concern etched on his forehead, I hold my hand up.

"Just leave me alone!"

Before he can say another word, I turn and move away from him as fast as I can in my heels, my stomach churning with nausea.

I reach the bathroom at the same time the house lights flare to life. My stomach heaving, I grab for the door handle just as a guy exits. Ignoring the gasps of outrage from the few girls waiting in line, I tug the door closed behind me and hold my hand over my mouth, stumbling to the toilet.

My stomach empties quickly, nothing but champagne, then dry heaves.

I shiver as hot and cold flashes up and down my body, but once the dry heaves stop, I manage to drag myself over to the sink to rinse my mouth out.

I've just turned off the tap when my gaze locks with Calder's steady one in the mirror. He's leaning against the wall directly behind me, arms crossed.

"Care to tell me what that disappearing act was about?"

As embarrassment heats my cheeks, I gesture to the toilet and what he obviously just now witnessed. My voice shakes as I answer, "Too much champagne apparently."

Without a word, he removes his hat and sets it on the counter, then steps behind me, his green gaze holding mine in the mirror. "Fifteen minutes have passed since you left me. And I find you on the other side of the fucking house? What the hell is—?"

I spin and wrap my arms around his waist. Pressing my face against his chest, I mumble, "I'm sorry, Calder. You—" I inhale deeply, dragging in his comforting smell. If I can't wipe out Jake's memory, I want to at least erase his smell. "—overwhelmed me. I've obviously had too much to drink tonight."

Calder tips my chin up, his warm gaze slowly sliding along my jaw and neck. "A lesser man would take advantage of you in this condition."

I sigh and close my eyes, then jerk them open when the room starts to spin. "One thing you aren't is a *lesser* man. Your stats remain unchallenged. You're still at one-hundred-percent. I need to find Scarlett so she can take me home."

Smirking, he wraps an arm around my waist as if he

doesn't want to let me go. "I can take you. Bash will bring Scarlett later."

I start to shake my head, then wince at the ringing the sudden movement causes. "No, we came together. I want her to take me home. Can you call Bash and see if he knows where she is?"

Someone knocks impatiently on the door while Calder calls Bash. I pop a mint in my mouth that I discover in the glass dispenser on the vanity, then open the door and say, "There's another bathroom near the back kitchen entrance. It's going to be a few minutes."

When the girl gives me a knowing, snarky look, it's on the tip of my tongue to tell her it's not what she thinks, but she and her girlfriends walk away before I can utter a word.

The second I shut and lock the door, Calder tugs me back into his arms. "They'll meet us at the door in a couple minutes."

I take his phone and add an old email to his notes app. He won't be able to trace it back to me, but a part of me can't let him go without a way to connect. "Just in case you want a note from home while you're away."

Smiling, he tucks his phone away in his pocket. When his gaze drops to my mouth, I start to step back, but his arm only cinches tighter around me.

"I thought you weren't a lesser man," I say lightly, even as my chest constricts with a mixture of apprehension and anticipation. I can't let him reel me in again. I might not be able to walk away this time.

Calder swipes his thumb across my bottom lip, his gaze following its path. "I have to know, Celeste."

"Raven," I correct.

His gaze meets mine. "Will *Raven* let me kiss her?"

I swallow and nod, wanting nothing more, yet fearing where it might lead.

Calder tucks his finger under my chin, then presses his mouth firmly, but gently against mine.

When he doesn't do anything more than that, I allow myself the brief luxury of melting against his hard frame. He feels so solid and safe, I can't help it.

His warm breath bathes my lips as his fingers slide into my hair. "I want to be a lesser man right now. So fucking much," he mutters just before his lips claim mine.

His kiss parts my lips with possessive intensity, the erotic glide of his tongue provoking and enticing as he consumes every breath. Slanting his mouth against mine, he delves intimately deep, showing me how he plans to have me—wholly, completely, and without reservation. It's so unfair that he's hitting me with a parting kiss that skips permission and goes straight for forgiveness, so I dig my fingers into his muscular back and return his kiss with equal intensity, determined he'll leave this bathroom just as affected.

The door handle rattles and a knock sounds as someone calls through the wood, "Anyone in there?"

I break our kiss and whisper against his mouth, "I'm sorry about tonight, Calder. You'll never know how much."

He runs his nose along my cheekbone, his erection

pressing between my legs. "Actually, I do." When I wince, he pulls back. "The next time I kiss you, I won't stop until I'm sliding inside you as deep as I can get." Clasping my jaw, he lifts me to my toes, his serious gaze scanning my face. "No masks, no costumes. No fake names. No *fake* anything. Just you and me, and unending pleasure and sweat."

The sincerity in his vow turns me to mush while at the same time crushing my heart. I hate that he's making promises to an imposter. "Calder, I can't—"

"Hey...can you hurry up. I've got to go," the girl calls as she knocks impatiently.

Calder presses his forehead to mine. "Your friend is probably at the door by now."

CHAPTER SEVEN

CALDER

The moment she sees Scarlett, Celeste throws herself into her friend's arms. "Scarlett, tague me home. I feewl awfuz."

Bash instantly cuts an accusing gaze my way. I just shake my head and shrug. *What the hell?* "She sounds a lot more drunk than she did a minute ago, man," I say under my breath.

Once we follow them outside and I see a cab waiting, my concern for Celeste raises. "Doesn't she have a driver?"

"Oh, she's staying with me tonight, so no driver. We decided to taxi it," Scarlett says, looking flustered while trying to make sure Celeste doesn't hit her head getting into the cab.

As I watch Bash lean on the open car door trying to convince Scarlett to let him ride along with them, I can tell he's as frustrated as I feel. Of course she turns him down, but when he lifts Scarlett's hand and kisses the inside of her palm, my gaze narrows. So he's not *quite* as frustrated as me. *Lucky fucker.* At least one of us won't go home with blue balls tonight.

Then again, of the two of us, he deserves to get laid more. The guy is entirely too intense. Though I'm surprised he connected with someone at a party. This kind of hookup isn't his scene. But he did go toe-to-toe with Gavin earlier, so he's not acting entirely out of character. A smirk tugs at my lips. Scarlett must have an amazing body underneath that costume to draw Bash out of the shadows.

When the cab drives away, Bash stares after it for a couple of seconds, then claps me on the shoulder. "Let's head inside. I need to check on Mina now that she's decided to join the party."

"You going to tell me about that?" I ask, nodding after the car's taillights.

"*That's* none of your damn business," he says, walking away.

His curt tone makes me laugh as I follow him inside.

Apparently, Celeste's quick departure has drawn a crowd. The group of gawkers move away from the glass on either side of the door as Bash and I walk in. The sight of them ogling ticks me off. Scowling, I bark out, "Nothing to see here. Get back to the party."

Bash slides me a sideways look as we pass through the crowd and move further into the main room. "Settle down, Cald."

I start to say something about despising gossipmongers

when a blond guy dressed as a gladiator steps into my path. "I've never seen Celeste so out-of-it before. What'd you do to her?"

A couple inches shorter than my six-two height, the guy might be a year or so younger than me, but his accusation raises my protective instincts. I clench my fists by my side and vaguely hear Bash tell me to walk away. "Celeste is fine and none of your concern," I manage to say in an even tone.

The gladiator puffs his muscular chest up like a peacock, his gaze slitting. "You don't recognize me without my helmet, do you?"

Helmet? What the hell is he rambling about? Wait...football? "Are you talking about high school?" I've killed men with no names, but whose faces will remain etched in my mind until I take my last breath. I've been attacked by men wielding knives, bullets, and explosives. I've seen best friends go through PTSD, lose their limbs, their lives, and plenty of other dark shit I'd prefer to forget. For a split-second, I just stare incredulously at this jackass, who lives in his safe, elitist bubble. Shaking my head, I move to walk around him.

He sidesteps back into my path and folds his arms. "That's right," he says, tilting his chin at an arrogant angle. "Even as a sophomore I kicked your team's ass. Celeste is mine. Stay away from her."

"Calder—"

Just as Bash starts to put a staying hand on my shoulder, my fist connects with the fucker's smug face as I grit out, "Celeste knows who's worth spending her time with."

The guy hits the floor hard, skidding across the wood. Everyone backs away and stops talking to watch as the idiot jumps to his feet. Swiping blood from his upper lip, he shouts, "Do you know who the hell I *am?*"

"Do you think I give two *fucks?*" Hearing him talk about Celeste like she's his makes my blood boil. I want to smear this guy's face into the ground. I take an aggressive step toward him, but Bash grabs my arm.

"Not here, Cald. He's not worth it."

Chest heaving, fists clenched, the guy seethes. "I'm Jake Hemming. My father is a senior partner at Hemming, Gersh, and Platt."

"And I'm Calder *fucking* Blake. Might want to write that down so you don't forget it when you go whining to your lawyer daddy."

Jake's face flushes even as his hazel gaze turns cold. "We'll ruin you." Glancing around at those gawking, he gestures to me. "You all are witnesses. He attacked me."

My adrenaline vaults and as the beast inside me roars to be set free, the steel hold on my arm tightens. "I didn't see anything," Bash states calmly, then addresses the onlookers. "Did anyone see what happened?"

One by one, they mumble in the negative, then turn back to their drinks and chatting with friends.

"Are you serious?" Jake snaps, glancing around for support.

Gavin approaches, his mouth pressed in a tight line. Eyeing Bash's hand on my arm with a hard glare, he turns to Jake. "I think it's time for you to leave."

Bash releases me as Jake's eyes widen in disbelief. "You're fucking kidding me, right?"

Gavin's dark gaze hardens behind his mask. "You don't come into *my* home and cause problems with my family. I'm not going to ask you again."

Once Jake storms out, Gavin sighs heavily at Bash and me. "Do you two think you can control yourselves the rest of the evening? I'd actually like to enjoy the party."

Bash shrugs. "I never make promises I can't keep."

"I'll keep him out of trouble," I say, choking back a laugh at Bash's honest response.

Gavin shakes his head and slides his hands in his dress pants pockets, his voice dropping to private mode. "It's a good thing you're both heading out soon." Fixing his gaze on Bash, he continues, "The Blake name can only stretch so far to cover your asses—"

"We got it," I cut him off in a cold tone, my amusement gone in defense of Bash. I'm the one who nearly started a fight, yet he's getting the blame.

Once Gavin walks away, I shake my head. "Gavin can be such a—"

"Dick," Bash supplies.

I'll never understand how Bash can be so unaffected. I want to pummel Gavin each time a dig comes out of his mouth. Then again, Bash's control over his emotions is one of the things I admire most about my cousin. He's taught me a lot in that regard. He might be Gavin and Damien's illegitimate half-brother, but I'm closer to him than they'll ever be.

It's a fucking shame that Mina is the only one who returns Bash's sibling loyalty.

Raising an eyebrow, Bash smirks. "Care to tell me what that was all about with Jake? These last few years, I've seen you take far more shit without losing it."

I know he switched the subject on purpose. Bash is a master at redirection. Instead of calling him on it, I let it go. But I'm sure as hell not talking to him about Celeste. Whatever's going on there is too new. All I know is that I wanted to pile-drive that asshole into the ground for even thinking about touching her. "That's none of your damn business." Ignoring his knowing chuckle, I nod toward the bar. "Go check on Mina, then come sit with me while I drown my sanctioned good behavior in a mug of beer."

CHAPTER EIGHT

CASS

Talia's thrashing around wakes me. I blink quickly, my brain foggy and sluggish. It's four a.m. I'm surprised I'm in her bed. I don't remember much about the car ride home other than teasing her that I hope she got laid. I definitely don't remember her getting me into the house. She must've brought me to her room so she could keep an eye on me. I will always miss my sister, but Talia has made the hole in my heart feel less empty.

When she suddenly elbows my arm, I bite back the cry of pain. Her restrained wails and twitchy movements make my heart ache, but I wait until she rolls to her side, then I quickly wrap my arm around her and hold her in place, calling in her ear, "It's a nightmare, Talia!"

She flips onto her back, her breath heaving in and out. I gently touch her cheek. "You're okay. I'm right here." When

I see tears trickle down her temple I brush them away. "It's okay."

The first time this happened in our dorm room, it freaked me out. But I understood nightmares, so I crawled into bed with her until she calmed down. I think she appreciated that I never asked what tormented her sleep. But now...after all this time. I'm a bit worried. I wait until she settles, then say, "You haven't had one of those in a while. Do you want to talk about it?"

She grabs my hand and rolls back over, taking my arm with her. "No."

I recognize her avoidance, but I can also sympathize so I just snuggle close. "One of these days you're going to tell me."

She immediately slides her fingers across the scars on my wrist. "Just like you'll tell me, right?"

It takes effort not to pull from her touch, but I hold steady, remaining silent. She sighs and tugs me closer. "I love you, Cass, but you still smell like a bar."

I snicker and brush my lips against her cheeks, purposely blowing my horrid breath across her face. When she protests and tries to roll away, I just grasp her tighter, knowing she needs a comforting touch despite our goofiness. This is exactly what my sister would've done for me, and I'm glad I'm here for Talia.

I can feel the tension vibrating in her body, so I whisper, "Think about the fact you finally got laid instead. Hold on to the positive thoughts."

She instantly goes still against me. "How did you know that?"

I run my tongue across my lips, licking the salt I tasted when my mouth touched her cheek. "Because you smell like cologne and taste like sweat." Just to rev her up once more, I lick her whole cheek and laugh when she gags and attempts to swat me away. "And because you wouldn't tell me. That's how I know."

Her silence makes me wonder if she's still thinking about her dream, so I try to draw her thoughts away. "Why don't you tell me what happens this afternoon at four instead?"

"You heard that?" she whispers.

I snort. "I was drunk, not deaf."

"Just coffee," she sighs.

"Good!" Relieved she's started to relax, I bury my nose against the back of her neck. "And I love you too, Talia."

After we lay there in quiet silence for a bit and I finally hear her breathing even out in untroubled sleep, my heart feels lighter with the knowledge Talia finally had sex. Maybe it will help her stop obsessing so much on the newspaper. She's entirely too focused and never allows herself any time for fun. At least one of us got the full-shebang of wonderful feelings tonight.

Well, what I could only *imagine* wonderful feelings would feel like to fully let yourself go with someone. To be completely uninhibited. Maybe the mask and fake name helped her get past her hang-ups about guys not being good enough. Bash certainly seemed like a fine specimen.

As happy as I am for her, a part of me twinges with jealousy. I desperately wish I had the freedom to spend the night with Calder, to find out if that amazing orgasm I experienced with him was just a one time thing. *Could I really let myself go with him?* But unlike Talia, who could completely hide behind her anonymity tonight, I came to the party as someone else behind my mask and had to maintain that underlying persona. No matter how much it killed me.

Crawling out of bed, I stumble to the bathroom. I'm still in my costume. Well, minus the heels. As the light pops on, I flip my dark, rat-nested hair out of my eyes to stare in the mirror. I'm tired and bleary-eyed, but even looking a bit haggard, I have perfectly spaced eyes, nice lips, and symmetrical bone-structure. Perfect from a photographer's perspective. Some would call me pretty. Just like Celeste.

I scowl at the image.

Not only did Celeste cost me Calder tonight, she cost me my inner peace. Jake would've smirked at Cass if he happened to run into her tonight, but otherwise he would've pretended she didn't exist. Coming face-to-face with him shook me more than I thought it would. I wasn't prepared for the full deluge of self-disgust that hit the moment he touched me.

I didn't throw up because I was drunk like I let Calder believe. Jake makes my skin feel like it's teaming with bugs and my stomach dip and rise like a seesaw. The sheer dislike rocketing through me flushed my cheeks and made it hard to breathe. I loathe him with every fiber of my being. I can't believe that I ever thought he was attractive. I hate that what he did to me fucked with my mind, twisting me inside out. If I could've flattened him with my fist, I would've right there in front of everyone. But I wasn't me. I was Celeste. *Proper. Bitchy. Spoiled.* And put on a pedestal by him.

I scowl at the face in the mirror that has caused me so much grief, then hit the light switch, cutting off the image.

My phone buzzing with an alert draws my attention just as I start to crawl back into bed. I grab it from Talia's nightstand so it doesn't wake her, my heart rate jumping when I see it's from Calder.

FROM: Mr. Navy
　　To: Raven089276@boxmail.com
　　Come fly with me, Raven. I promise to keep you warm.

BITING MY LIP, I send him a message back.

FROM: Raven
　　I shouldn't have to remind you that you're Navy, not Air Force.

FROM: Mr. Navy
　　I'm also a qualified pilot. I promise I'm fully capable of taking you to the mile-high club.

· · ·

MY HEART RACES. I already miss his sexy arrogance. The promises he made just before I had to leave echo in my mind, twisting my stomach in excitement despite the fact it will never happen. He caught me off guard in so many ways. Even though there's no guarantee he'd be able to repeat the experience I had with him tonight, if circumstances were different, I'd want to let him try.

Maybe...once he gets back from deployment in a year or so, I can find a way to bump into him *as me*. I shake my head when I realize that I don't even know his last name. *But if I stalk Celeste's social media, I'll bet someone will mention him in connection to her after tonight.* Sadly the last thing I want to do is watch the gossip firestorm now. I quickly delete the social media app from my phone so I'm not tempted. My fantasy of running into Calder as me will have to remain just that. Even in that scenario, I would be lying to him all over again. My heart is heavy as I send him a note back.

FROM: Raven

You're a man of many talents. Who knew you were so multifaceted? Sadly, I can't come out to play.

FROM MR. NAVY

Then I'll come to you.

· · ·

PANIC SEIZES MY CHEST. If he shows up at the Carver's estate, I'm toast. I quickly type an email back.

FROM: Raven

I can't. Sorry. I have to keep an eye on Scarlett. She's not feeling well.

FROM: Mr. Navy

Then if I'm stuck here awake by myself, tell me something about you. What are you going to do when you graduate from college?

MY FINGERS PAUSE over my phone's keyboard. I could lie and talk about going into business like my father wants me to, but instead I share what's lived only in my heart. Something no one else knows.

FROM: Raven

I'm going to travel the world, creating imagery that takes your breath away and makes you wish you were there.

As soon as I hit send, I make a mental note to switch to Columbia's Visual Arts program on Monday. I'm going to do it...follow my passion for photography. I'm surprised when he doesn't immediately fire back a response, even if it's just to tease me about sounding so fanciful. The silence carries its own message. My heart sinking, I know it's for the best, so I send him one last note to let him off the hook.

DEAR CALDER,

I GUESS this is my farewell letter to you before your deployment. Be safe wherever you're going and take care of yourself.

RAVEN

CHAPTER NINE

CASS

Four Years Later

WHILE MOST PEOPLE think in terms of years, as a photographer, I think in blocks of time. Seasons to be exact. Four seasons in a year; four opportunities to shine. For me, the composition of my fashion shoots—the colors and designs chosen—centers around seasonal changes. The seasons play a big part in how and where I plan my next photo session around the world. And yeah, the need to travel to places I've never seen is a small piece of that decision too.

Non-stop traveling has been my modus operandi since college; that is until my mom came down with mono. And as much I teased her like crazy about getting "the kissing disease"—after the doctors took several weeks to rule out much worse ailments—I was just relieved she was diagnosed with something she could recover from. Antibiotics and loads of rest was the doctors' prescribed cure.

My father is a great man when it comes to running his business development company and providing for our family, but he's the worst nurse ever. So I've spent the last three months tending to my mom at our Hamptons home. I already lost one family member. I sure as hell wasn't going to lose another.

I truly love my mom, but now that she's almost a hundred percent, I'm getting antsy to get back into the excitement of a new project that I can really dig my teeth into. I'll never admit to anyone that I've enjoyed the leisure of not *having* to travel these last few months, but being unable to take pictures daily has been like losing a limb. I lost count of the number of times I reached for a camera, then sighed with sadness that my equipment was packed away.

Viewing life through a lens, adjusting it and making it better so everyone can see the perfection...it's my own kind of therapy. I don't expect to have a fairytale *anything* in my life, not with my issues, so I create visuals that feel that way. Now that I have some extra time to myself, I've spent the last few days driving around the Hamptons and refilling my photography well full of landscapes, waterscapes, and general "life in the Hamptons" shots. It's a far cry from my normal glitzy shots, but oddly comforting. With all the photos I've taken in the Hamptons, an idea for a destination location book has already started to percolate.

I'd gotten up extra early this morning, hoping to capture the best sunrise shots. The water was smooth with just a few ripples, perfect for reflection imagery. I managed to grab some amazing pictures, but as the sun continued to rise and the golden light began to bounce off the water like glitter scattered across its smooth surface, memories of Calder and me made it too hard to think. I tried to move on to other areas I planned to shoot for the day, but thoughts of Calder followed me, stealing my ability to concentrate. *What is he doing? Where did he go once he came back to New York?*

My focus blown for the day, I drive into town to clear my head and grab some coffee. When my phone rings, I push the button on my dash and put it on speaker. "Hey," I say, while approaching the town's shopping district.

"Well, hello stranger," Talia says. "Long time no talk. How's your mom?"

I turn on my blinker, and stop to let a guy on a bike cross the street. "Mom's doing much better. Thanks for asking."

"That's wonderful. I'm so glad. And what are you doing right now?" She continues in a bright tone.

"Um, I'm working."

A snort. "I hear your blinker ticking. You're not taking pictures at the moment. Guess where I am?" She doesn't even take a breath before she blurts out, "I'm at our Hamptons house! Come have lunch with me."

Pushing on the gas, I turn another corner, then pull into The Grinder's parking lot and cut the engine. "I really am working, Talia. Maybe some other time."

"You've said that the last three weekends I've invited you here. When are you going to forgive me?"

I take my phone off speaker and put it to my ear. "Not that I'm holding a grudge, but I'm pretty sure it's bad form to get married without at least having your best friend present." Though I am a bit hurt Talia ran off and married Sebastian—apparently "Bash" was Calder's nickname for him—I'm having a much harder time with the idea of visiting the Hamptons house Sebastian purchased as a gift to Talia. While it might hold wonderful memories for them as the place they first connected at that party, that's not the case for me. Too many regrets rise to the surface when I think about the place I met Calder.

"Cass, it was just the judge, Sebastian, and me. I'm sorry that my doing so hurt your feelings, but my family situation is still up in the air. I'm not even sure who I would've invited to sit on my side if we'd had a traditional wedding in a church."

I feel bad for making her reopen old wounds about her family. "I'm sorry, Talia. Please don't think I don't want to spend time with you. I've just been swamped with my mom's stuff."

"Well, at least she's doing much better. That should give you some breathing room to start being social again soon. Speaking of being social...have you heard from Calder yet?"

My fingers curl around the edge of my phone, my stomach churning. "No, which is the same answer the last four times you asked me."

Talia sighs. "I thought for sure when he asked me to

94

apologize to you—well Celeste—for not writing back, and I suggested he contact you to reconnect, that he would. He seemed genuinely sincere."

I feel so lame for secretly holding out hope Calder would eventually contact me that my defensive sarcasm rises to the surface. "It's been over three months since you saw him at Mina's baby's christening. And considering none of Calder's family has seen or heard from him since then, I think we can safely assume at this point that he's not going to contact me. *Please* stop asking me. I'm starting to get a complex."

I keep my tone light, which is so far from how I feel about Calder Blake. Yeah, that *Blake,* as in...he's from one of the wealthiest families in the country. Learning Calder was a Blake from Talia had been a major "You've got to be kidding me" moment, considering I spent the entire evening at that party thinking he only had his military career going for him.

"I'm sorry, Cass. I'm sure it's not you. Sebastian said that Calder's father dying right after the party really did a number on him. It's driving Sebastian crazy that even with his security resources he hasn't been able to find his cousin. Maybe I should've told Calder the truth about who you are when he and I talked briefly that day? That might've intrigued him into wanting to get to know the real you."

"I doubt telling Calder I was really someone else would've helped, Talia." *It probably would've made him hate me, considering how he feels about being lied to.* Then again, which is worse: being ignored due to disinterest, or being hated due to disgust? Either option sucks and apparently ends with the same result. Silence.

"I actually think the truth would be better coming from you," Talia says.

I wave my hand, clearing the invisible cloud over my head. "This is all a moot point, so let's change the subject. How about a marriage party?"

"A what?"

"I'm suggesting that you and Sebastian throw a party, where all your friends get to eat, drink, dance, and toast to your marriage."

"Hmmm, that sounds like a great idea. Maybe we can have it here."

My stomach sinks and I quietly smack my forehead. "Or maybe in Manhattan?"

"I'll talk to Sebastian and see what he thinks. He'll probably want to have it here. Thanks for the suggestion."

"Sure. Well, I've got to get back to work."

"Oh, okay. I've got some phone calls to make anyway. I've got a lead on an article I just got assigned. How about next time you call me for lunch plans. Friendship works both ways, Miss Cass."

"But of course," I say with a laugh before hanging up. I know I've been the worst friend lately. I'll blame it on the extra long-winter keeping me hibernating at home, but now that we're having some spring-like days, I'll have to get over it. I really am thrilled that at least one of us benefited from attending that masked party. Sebastian turned out to be a keeper, even if it took Talia and him a while to finally get together. Talk about stubborn. Then again, who am I kidding? I'm *still* single, so my best friend has one-upped me in that area.

I walk into The Grinder's cozy café, shivering at the brisk March air chasing me inside. Unlike yesterday's sixty-seven high, today the temperature has only reached fifty. After ordering a latte, I find an empty corner table and hook my shoulder bag on my chair. Setting my camera on the table, I pull the latest issues of Vogue and Harper's Bazaar from my bag and sit down, preparing to indulge.

Okay, I'll be honest...I'm scoping out the competition. Three months out of the biz is a lifetime. An entire season... gone. I have to catch up and start planning my next shoot. I really need to get invigorated again.

I feast on the vivid spring colors as I flip the pages in the March issue, pausing on a section on Monaco. The feature highlights gorgeous women draped in jewels and flowing gowns, and striking men sporting custom tuxes as they lean against luxury cars known for their speed. Of course the breathtaking Mediterranean views make the perfect back-drop. With each new scene, the photographer did a fantastic job conveying the opulent lavishness and fairytale life in the French Riviera.

When I reach the middle of the magazine, an advertise-ment with the cityscape of Manhattan stretches across both pages. Pausing, I smile at my home. I love Manhattan. It has its own glitz and glamour, and its grit and dark places too. I run my fingers across the glossy pages, tracing the skyline. The idea of photographing Manhattan like I've captured the

Hamptons these past few days really appeals. Not just the city, but the people, the venues. No one can capture it better than someone who lives and breathes it.

Real life. Not fairytales.

"Still dreaming of the glitzy life, Cass Rockwell?" Celeste says breezily. Sitting in the chair across from me, she picks up the Vogue magazine and opens it with a flourish.

While her expensive perfume adds to the heaviness of her presence, I straighten my spine and exhale harshly. She has no idea that that March issue of Vogue features some of my past work. Granted, no one but Talia knows that I'm the well-known fashion photographer *Raven* listed in the credits. Even on my website, I'm wearing sunglasses. And while I usually prefer to keep it that way, when Celeste stops turning pages to stare at the centerfold spread of the exclusive beach party I shot in Barcelona, a small part of me wants to say, "Now I inspire *your* fashion sense," but I just press my lips together and say nothing.

Right now all I see is the top of Celeste's glossy dark hair, big curls spilling across the shoulders of her cashmere coat. I recognize the coat designer's style, but I don't bother acknowledging her vanity. She might not be looking at me, but the quick way she moves on to other pages in the magazine, flipping too fast to really see anything, tells me she's using it as a distraction. When she glances up at me, a memory of her pausing at the end of the aisle in the school library to stare at me where I sat on the floor near the window with an oversized book in my lap, blips through my mind.

"Shhhhhhh," Our high school librarian, Mrs. Heart, shushed Celeste and her friend as they giggled. They were supposed to be in the library researching their projects for our art history class.

At the same time I looked up, Celeste's gaze landed on me. It had been a year since the incident with Jake at Shelley's party. A year since I'd lost my sister. A year since I started wearing cuff bracelets of any kind: leather, cloth, silver, stainless steel, beaded, brass. All that mattered was the width. Two inches wide. My clothes had to change with my new accessories, so I adopted a kind of a retro hip, grunge look. And even though I couldn't bring myself to cut my hair —my sister would be horrified—I always wore it up in a messy claw-clipped bun. Anything to keep me from looking like Celeste and off Jake's radar.

Apparently I'd started a trend among the girls in my grade. Bracelets on both wrists became the new "it" accessory. Sometimes matching. Sometimes mismatched. Not that I cared. I spent all my time in the library. It was the one place I knew I'd never run into Jake.

Approaching me, Celeste chuckled when she saw the fashion designs and color swatches depicted on the pages. Squatting down, she flipped to the front of the book and read the title out loud, "Colored by Design." Opening the cover, she glanced at the copyright year. "Nineteen-sixty-five. Really Cass?" Standing, she shook her head and folded her arms. "I have more fashion sense then that musty old book. If you want tips, I just attended fashion week over spring break."

I didn't want to draw or design the clothes, but I loved

P. T. MICHELLE

studying the set ups. It helped me visualize seeing how the clothes, jewelry, and even the backgrounds, when put together via color and placement, set the whole scene and brought it to life.

While the fair-skinned, pencil thin cheerleader next to Celeste snickered, I noticed the thick gold bangles on Celeste's wrists. Of course hers were expensive and purely to display her wealth. I wanted to rail at her...to blame her for what happened to me, but as far as I knew Celeste didn't know what Jake did to me at Shelley's party. No one did, other than the unknown asshole who participated with Jake.

I still had no clue who that was. But God forbid Jake's goddess would discover what a true bastard he could be. My fingers twitch around the edges of the book. Telling her wouldn't do any good; she has never given him the time of day. For all I know, she might be twisted enough to find what he did to me amusing. All I can think about is going home and sliding something sharp along the inside of my wrist. With the pain, blissful release always follows. Something other than constant numbness is a welcome experience.

"*So, would you like to hear about the latest Paris fashions?*"

Hearing "Paris" pulled me out of my dark thoughts. I blinked at her and shook my head. "I'll just faux pas my way to a fashion sense."

Flipping her long hair over her shoulder, Celeste sniffed her irritation, obviously unused to someone rebuffing her. "Suit yourself. I was only trying to help."

As she walked away, I mumbled, "Your help is the last thing I'll ever need."

Celeste snapping her fingers in front of me yanks me back to the present. "Are you living in your glamorous world right this second?" she says, a slight smirk on her lips.

"Nah, I'm just slumming it here in the Hamptons," I deadpan. *What the hell does she want? I haven't spoken to her since high school.*

A half dozen thin gold bangles clink against a dainty jeweled aquamarine bracelet as she hands me the magazine. "You always were a smartass."

I blink in surprise. *When did she start cursing?*

Before I can speak, the waitress, who's wearing retro horn-rimmed glasses and a small scarf tie around her high ponytail, stops by our table. "Would you like to order a coff—"

When she cuts herself off, her gaze pinging between us, Celeste smiles, clearly amused. "I'll have a decaf latte."

I shake my head while the girl jots down Celeste's order on a notepad without taking her gaze from us. I'm wearing jeans, a navy zip-up sweat jacket, and no makeup. I've also been traipsing around taking pictures in the morning mist, so my hair has to be a mess of waves. I seriously doubt we look that much alike right now.

As the waitress walks away, I notice the girl's saddle shoes and rolled up jeans. *Is it retro day at the café or is rockabilly making a comeback here in this pocket of the Hamptons?*

"So you're probably wondering why I'm here. " Celeste cuts into my attempt to ignore her presence.

"The thought crossed my mind," I say in a dry tone as I watch her absently fiddle with the gold charms on her delicate necklace. A golden lock, a key, and a diamond encrusted heart. Real diamonds. *How upper-crust cliché.*

She ignores my crisp comment and tilts her head, sliding her gaze over my face. "I've seen you taking pictures the last few days while I was in town shopping. You've stopped in here several times."

Note to self: no more habitual anything. *It makes you too easy to find.* "And now I'm entertaining the notion that you're stalking me." I hold Celeste's gaze, my own expression carefully schooled as I wait for her to reveal her agenda.

Taking a deep breath, she shrugs. "What? No, how's it going, Celeste? Or, what have you been up to since high school?"

"How's it going, Celeste?" I sound bored, even though I want to snap back, "Did you ask me?"

The waitress interrupts, dropping off Celeste's latte. Blowing on her coffee to cool it, Celeste looks at me and sighs. "You really don't like me, do you?"

"What gave me away?" I close my magazine and stack it on top of the other before slipping them both into my bag.

When I move to pick up my camera, Celeste puts a hand on my arm. "I'd like you to stay."

"We don't have anything to talk about." Pulling free of her hold, I set my camera in the bag.

Just as I heft the bag's strap onto my shoulder, she says in a sincere tone, "I need your help, Cass."

Shock turns my stomach upside down, but ramping tension quickly rights it. "What makes you think I would *want* to help you?"

Celeste folds her hands around the bottom of her cup. Lowering her voice, she leans forward. "Because you owe me."

Fury flashes and I quickly stand. "I don't owe you jack—"

"Sit down, Cass," Celeste cuts in, her casual tone suddenly serious. "You went to the Blakes' party as me that night."

"What party?" Not that I'm admitting anything, but I sink back into the chair out of curiosity. The tension in her face surprises me. I never did check on-line to see if there had been any fallout for Celeste.

Celeste's brown gaze turns laser sharp. "Look, I kept my mouth shut and took the shit your presence at that party caused in my life, and now I'd like you to help me."

Why did she keep her mouth shut? "The shit *I* caused in *your* life?" I speak slowly, trying my best not to scream at the girl. So maybe getting caught hooking up with a guy in the kitchen caused her some embarrassment and probably even a few party invitations for a while. Aw, that must've been such a tragedy to deal with in that ivory tower of hers.

Celeste shakes her head. "You have no idea. In return for my silence back then, I'm asking you to do me a favor."

My gaze narrows. "Are you trying to blackmail me?"

Her face flushes. "I wasn't exactly trying to—"

Snorting, I stand and put my hand on the table, leaning close. "A bit of advice, if you're going to blackmail someone, make sure it's for something they give a damn about."

Before she can reply, I walk out.

I've just unlocked my car door when Celeste says from behind me. "I'm sorry that I didn't phrase my request very well. I need you to be me, Cass. Just for a day."

Now she wants me to be her? I might be curious, but I'm not stupid. I open my car door.

"Please, Cass." Celeste reaches around me and pushes the door shut. "I really need your help. Do you think I would be here if I had any other choice?"

The desperation in her voice makes me pause. I've never known Celeste to *beg* for anything. I glance over my shoulder and am surprised at the dark circles under her eyes that her makeup can't hide in outside light.

"Why do you want me to impersonate you?"

Folding her hands together, Celeste says, "I don't know if you've been keeping up with politics, but my father's ramping up for his campaign run in the fall. This weekend, he's hosting a huge party at our house in Westchester to help him garner even more supporters. It's his time to shine and show off his family."

I knew her father had been appointed Senator last year when the previous Senator died of a sudden heart attack. A man with many varied holdings and businesses, prior to his appointment, Gregory Carver had contributed heavily to several political campaigns in previous years, garnering him loads of respect in the right circles. According to the news, he'd been well received as an appointee in the Senate, and now he's planning to run on his own merit.

I hold Celeste's gaze for a beat. "Sounds important. You really need to be there."

She nods her agreement. "That's the whole point. I have to be there for my dad, but I've waited weeks for this appointment. I can't miss it."

I'm already shaking my head. "It's one thing to fool partiers where everyone's half drunk and pretending to be someone else in masks and costumes, but there's no way—"

"Do you really think a political function is any different?" she cuts in with a laugh, her eyes lighting up for the first time. Sobering, she continues, "Seriously, it'll be fine, Cass. All you have to do is nod, shake hands, and say, 'It's nice to meet you', for an evening. That's it. When the event is over, you can say you're running an errand and we'll meet up somewhere and I'll take my car back."

Not that I'm really entertaining this, but I frown at her last comment. "Why would I need your car?"

"Oh," she waves like it's no big deal. "It'll be best if you get dressed for the evening in my room there at the estate, just like I would."

"I don't understand why you aren't in an apartment," I say, genuinely perplexed that she still lives at home.

"My father depends on me for a lot of hosting stuff, since my mom tires quickly. It's just easier for him if I live at home."

The idea of being in her personal space sends a shiver of "hell no" down my spine.

"Uh uh," I say, shaking my head. "Sorry, I can't do it." I quickly turn back to my car and open the door.

Just as I slide into my seat, she leans on my car door and says, "Not even to help your dad?"

CHAPTER TEN

CASS

"What are you talking about?" I ask, my gaze narrowing.

Celeste smiles. "I know your dad has been trying to get the zoning approval for his development expansion for a while. I might be able to help smooth the way for him."

My ears buzz with the jump in my heart rate. My father getting the city's approval would mean more than Celeste could ever know. It took me a couple years after Sophie's death to convince my dad to continue forward with his plans to expand his business.

Even though I was just as devastated to wake up the morning after my horrible experience with Jake to discover my sister had died, I knew why she'd taken a whole bottle of sleeping pills at once. Her cryptic comments the night before finally made sense. She didn't want her illness to ruin our family financially when her prognosis of surviving was so low. It took me a year to come to terms with her decision to leave us, and another ten months to help my father turn his guilt over her death into a mission to succeed no matter what.

Once my father got moving on his plans again, he went after the approval with all he had, but he kept hitting roadblocks with the zoning commission. He never gave up. Every year he tweaked his plan and every year he sought approval, only to be turned down. It got to the point, I dreaded when the opportunity rolled around for him each year. I always called that day, no matter where I was in the world. I knew exactly where he'd be—sitting in his office chair, proposal paperwork in the trash, a framed picture of Sophie in one hand, and a highball glass of Scotch in the other.

"Can you really help him get approved?"

Celeste lifts her shoulders. "I can't guarantee approval, but I can try."

Celeste might suck at blackmail, but she definitely knows how to dangle a carrot. "I see you're becoming a politician just like your father," I say, eyeing her skeptically.

Pressing her lips together, determination settles in her expression. "I'm familiar with what he's been trying to get approved. I will draft my support for him tonight. Tell Mr. Rockwell to set up an appointment to pitch his proposal next week if he wishes. Oh, and don't worry about the party, you won't be facing a *total* group of strangers at this event. Calder Blake will be there."

Just when I think things can't possibly get any worse than my nemesis dangling hope for my father in exchange for her help, she expects me to spend the evening—as *her*—with the only guy I've ever wanted?

Fuck my life.

"Calder?" I say casually, my heart racing at the mere mention of his name.

Celeste straightens and props her arm on the top of the car door. "Yeah, I guess I have you to thank for introducing me to him...well, in a roundabout sort of way."

And now I know why I never heard from Calder. If he contacted the *real* Celeste, then that means he must've figured out I was an imposter. Despite the heaviness that settles on my chest, I keep my tone light. "So you two have become friends?" *Please don't tell me you're sleeping with him. Please. Just. Don't.*

Celeste smiles. "You know...of the few parties Calder and I have attended together, I never really *saw* him before. But when he stopped by my house to apologize for losing my contact information, we talked and just clicked. We had lunch together after that, and then..." she pauses and exhales a sigh. "He's delicious. I just want to bite that man every time I see him."

Shit...he lost my email? It's possible. Phones crash, get lost, stolen. And of course Celeste didn't bother to tell him she *wasn't* the one he was with that night. He has no idea he's dating a different person. I'll bet she orgasms with him all the time. *Ugh, stop thinking about them having sex.* The idea makes me nauseous. Turning my gaze straight ahead, I grip the steering wheel and try to sound as disinterested as possible. "How great for you."

"It will be once I get this appointment taken care of."

What could possibly be so important that it can't wait a few days? Actually, the answer isn't my concern. "Well, it seems you're none-the-worse for my part in your past, especially now that you've got a new man in your life because of it."

Celeste nods. "Calder's the *only* good thing to walk into my life lately. And seeing how he had his face in your *crotch* at the party, I'm pretty sure you'll have no problem hosting him (platonically, of course) when he comes to the event on Saturday night to meet my father."

The fact she's reminding me not to screw her boyfriend while acting like what happened between Calder and me was just a trashy tryst, makes me grind my back teeth. Blinking back the sudden moisture in my eyes, I exhale an unsteady breath. The brief encounter I had with Calder meant *everything* to me. It meant I wasn't a fucked-up, dispassionate freak. He showed me that buried somewhere inside me, I have the capacity to be a warm, involved lover. Too bad it hasn't happened with anyone else since. He might be *my* solution, but apparently Celeste is his.

There's no guarantee she'll actually be able to help my dad, but there's a one-hundred-percent guarantee that the thought of Celeste and Calder together will torture me all night long. There is only so much I can take, and I've just reached my limit.

"Congrats all the way around, Celeste. Good luck with life and all."

I lean over to tug the door closed, my action forcing

Celeste back so she doesn't get crushed. I ignore her protests, completely tuning her out, but when my gaze lands on the tattooed word running along the inside of my outstretched forearm, I freeze.

Never.

It's in a script font with trailing ends before and after the word. I'd gotten it to remind me *never* to give in to my cravings to cut again, and to never give up on *me.*

But isn't that what I'm doing by saying 'no?' Am I really going to pass up the one and only chance I might get to tell Calder the truth?

Meeting Celeste's panicked gaze, I blow out a breath "Okay, I'll help you."

"Really?" Her whole face lights up and she grabs my arm. "Thank you so much, Cass. Tell your father to make that appointment." Releasing me, she smiles and clasps her hands excitedly. "Can you meet me here on Friday morning at nine? I'll give you all the details you'll need to know: pictures of family, employees, names, house layout, etc. Then we'll set a time and place for you to pick up my car."

Memorizing faces, who's who and how I should know them, and an entire estate's layout twenty-four hours before the event sounds *complicated.* There are so many ways I can trip myself up. I take a deep breath. *Helping your dad and also owning up to the past with Calder will be worth it, Cass.* Whether Calder forgives me or not remains to be seen, but at least I'll have given it my best shot. "I can meet you on Friday," I say, giving a firm nod.

"Great. I'll see you then." Celeste starts to walk away,

but then quickly turns back. "Oh, one more thing. I've asked Calder to consider becoming my personal guard. I think he needs a little more convincing. He insisted on meeting my father, so this event is the perfect time for that. My father's a tough sell on the idea, so it'll help loads if you talk with him about Calder before the event to prepare him to meet my suggested new guard. I think once Father meets him, he'll agree. Calder's SEAL training certainly speaks for itself."

SEAL? He's a freaking Navy SEAL? The fact I don't know this says just how little I really know about Calder. Not that he was forthcoming with the information that night at the party, but I can't believe Talia didn't mention it. Then again, I haven't talked to her about Calder, except for when she told me he might try to get in touch, and even then I acted laidback about it. My wandering thoughts suddenly stall as the implication of Celeste having a security person finally sinks in. "You *need* a bodyguard?"

"All the Carvers have a personal guard," Celeste says, shrugging. "But I'll admit to feeling as if someone's been following me for a while. That's why I think a new security person could be a good thing. Maybe a fresh set of eyes won't gloss over my daily life surroundings. My current guard sucks. Anyway, back to the event. I can't stress this enough—you mustn't tell anybody what you're doing for me, and under no circumstances can you reveal to anyone in my circle who you really are, including Calder, or this deal is off. Too much is riding on this. Do you understand?"

My heart sinks that her last directive rips away the deciding reason I agreed to this craziness in the first place. I had a glimmer of hope that Calder might possibly be able to forgive one deception, but now that I have to keep my mouth shut, that'll be twice I've lied to him. If Celeste didn't seem genuinely stressed about something, I'd think *this* was her ultimate revenge for me embarrassing her at that party.

I might be screwed, but for Celeste's help with my dad, I have to keep my word. "I understand, Celeste. I'll meet you here on Friday morning."

As I drive away, I question my sanity. I mean...how desperate does it make me that even though Calder will never know me as Cass, I can't wait to see him again? I refuse to think about it and instead dial my dad.

"How's my baby girl? Have you filled up your digital card already?" Dad asks, chuckling.

"Hey, Dad. I've been working, but I also realized what time of year it is. Isn't this your proposal time? I know you were thinking of skipping it this year, but I have a feeling this will be *your* year. And this time around, I'll be here to celebrate with you."

"Okay, I've locked the door. Now strip," Celeste says as she turns away from The Grinder's bathroom door and quickly steps out of her red-bottomed heels, then unzips her designer dove grey slacks. Lifting the bottom of her light blue cashmere sweater, she pauses and eyes me with an expectant look.

This is for Dad, I tell myself as I follow Celeste's instructions and tug off my cable knit cream-colored sweater. While Celeste spins her hand to move me along, I step out of my moto boots and quickly follow it up with my black leggings and miniskirt.

Holding her sweater in front of her, Celeste gestures to my bra.

I groan. "Is that really necessary?"

"Do *you* shop at Belle Femme?" She tilts her head impatiently.

I scowl. "I prefer not to spend a half a month's salary on matching underwear."

Huffing, she points to my nude bra. "The lace on that will be bulky through the sweater. Switch with me. Oh, by the way, I bought you a set that should work with the dress I'm supposed to wear tonight. You'll find the dress on the far left in my closet and the bra and panty set in the very top of my underwear drawer."

I don't even know how to respond to that. Saying "thank you" for buying me underwear just seems beyond weird—not that *this* scenario is normal at all—so I just put my back to her and unhook my bra, muttering, "At least I'll match." Handing my bra back to her, I say, "I draw the line at underwear."

"Ew, me too," she says as she replaces her bra with the one in my hand.

Once I hook her bra on, I sigh that the cups are a half size larger and slip the sweater over it. "You're um, a bit bigger than me." *Bet Calder loves that. Bleh.*

Celeste makes a pained sound behind me. "Your bra is

killing me. I'll have to stop and get one that fits. I figured you might be a little bit smaller than me. The set I bought should fit you."

Once we're dressed, Celeste turns me toward her and starts to mess with my hair. I tried to style it like hers before I left the house to meet her this morning, but my mom distracted me by asking what spurred me into encouraging my father to get his pitch ready to go.

The memory of hugging my dad and wishing him luck as he practiced his pitch for the committee just a couple hours ago flickers through my mind as I stand still for Celeste. My emotions swing wildly, making me feel light-headed. Or maybe it's Celeste's high-end perfume tickling my nose and the fact I'm wearing clothes that cost more than my car that are adding to my angst. I still don't like her, but she's a means to an end. *How does this make you any better than her, Cass?*

I ignore the flush that tightens my skin as I stare into "my face" up close.

Many mythologies have a spirit-double story, but considering my past interactions with Celeste, the one legend that keeps playing over-and-over in my mind is the German doppelgänger one. The myth foretells of an ill omen of impending death if you ever lay eyes on your "twin." *So what happens when you actually* become *her?* As tension ratchets within me, I push my sleeves up to help ward off the unsettled feeling and remind myself once more that I'm only here to make sure Dad fulfills his dream. I refuse to let

Sophie's sacrifice be for nothing. Not if I can do something about it.

Sliding her hands down my arms, Celeste clasps my wrists and lifts my arms away from my body, announcing, "Let's have a look at you."

Her smile fades as her perusal halts on the *Never* tattoo on my arm. When she starts to pull my wrists together, so she can stare at the raven sitting on the branch on one wrist and the continuing branch and vines on the other, my back stiffens.

Before I can pull away, she rubs her thumbs over the ink and obviously feels the scars hidden beneath. "Is this why you always wore bracelets in high school?" Deeper questions swirl among the surprise and sympathy in her eyes.

Jerking my arms free, I quickly pull my sweater's sleeves down. I refuse to be pitied. "Do I pass inspection?"

Nodding, she clears her throat. "You'll have to keep your tattoos covered. Thankfully my dress for the event is long-sleeved." She touches my hair, a slight smirk tilting her lips. "I have it on good authority that the deep ruby color will go well with your coloring."

I wrap my hands around my upper arms, suddenly chilled. "I know we've gone over everyone's names and such, but I'm worried I'm going to slip up. Do I really need to talk to your dad about Calder before the party?"

She quickly nods. "Father will be too distracted at the party to give the subject the attention it needs. It's important for you to prepare him to meet Calder."

When I blow out a steadying breath, she folds her hands

over mine around my arms. "You'll be fine. Just make sure you're not alone with anyone else prior to the party. That should lessen the chance you'll say something that sounds off. Hang out in my bedroom or go for a walk in the gardens; they're quiet and secluded. At the party, no one should ask you anything too personal or detailed. And if someone asks you something you don't know, just pretend you have a sudden tickle in your throat. They'll be too busy asking if you want something to drink to realize that you didn't answer."

Taking a smaller zip-up bag out of her purse, she hands the empty purse to me. "My wallet with my ID is in there, and I've put a phone in the inside pocket for you. It's a clone of my phone. Keep it on vibrate and ignore texts and social media stuff. I'll respond to anything that needs to be answered immediately, and I'll send you a text if you need to know about it. Otherwise just text me if you need to get in touch."

She pulls off her gold bangle bracelets and slips them on my wrist. When she starts to take off the gold necklace around her neck, I shake my head. "The bracelets should be enough."

Ignoring me, she hooks the necklace around my neck. "I never go anywhere without this. It will definitely be noticed if I'm suddenly not wearing it."

A knock sounds at the door, making me jump. "Is anyone in there?" a woman calls through the thick wood.

"One second," Celeste says in a perky tone.

When she suddenly turns and hugs me, whispering in

P. T. MICHELLE

my ear, "Thank you, Cass. You have no idea how much this means to me," I stiffen. She actually seems a bit nice, which raises my suspicious hackles. Old habits are hard to break.

I awkwardly reply, "A deal's a deal. My father is working all weekend to be ready to deliver his proposal next week."

CHAPTER ELEVEN

CASS

I can only drive around aimlessly for so long before I have to head to the Carver's estate. If nothing else, I need to get acquainted with the place and practice pretending I belong there before I have to meet with her dad. The idea of talking to Gregory Carver one-on-one is freaking me the hell out. I'm going to screw this up. I won't be able to do it. He'll see right through me. *God help me.*

My hands start shaking, the closer I get to the house. It might be true that I've successfully impersonated Celeste before, but that was at a party. This is different. It's in her home and far more personal. I must be perfect because my success has consequences that reach beyond me.

I tighten my hands on the steering wheel and quickly pull off the road to take several deep breaths. What if the moment I walk in, they see through the façade and know I'm an imposter. I can't pull this off. I'm not their caliber. I'm *not* Celeste. I don't have her poise, her snobbery...her overall I'm-better-than-the-rest attitude. I need someone to talk me down from my fears, so I reach out to the one person who has always had my back.

"Hey, you're calling me." Talia sounds surprised. "Is everything okay?"

"Of course, silly," I say in an upbeat tone.

"I'm glad to hear it. So does this phone call mean you changed your mind and you're coming this weekend?"

I chuckle. "No, I have plans, but I would like your advice."

"Ask away. I'm just unloading groceries."

The rustling of bags being set on a counter sounds in the background, along with cabinet doors opening and closing. I roll my head from one shoulder to the other, unsure how to phrase what I want to ask, so I just blurt it out. "I thought I was over my past, but I'm suddenly having to face it again. Well, in a different sort of way. I thought I could do it, but now I don't know if I can."

"Oh man, Cass. Are you sure you can't come see me? Or I could come to you. Where are you? It sounds like you could use some face-to-face time."

"No, it's okay, Talia. This is something I need to do. I guess...I'd like to know if you ever had to go back to your past and how you handled it?"

The scrape of a chair being pulled out precedes Talia's sigh. "I did. And no I didn't enjoy revisiting that part of my life, but in my case it was unavoidable. As painful as it was though, I learned that sometimes you have to go back so that you can move forward. That it's the only way you can truly leave the past behind you. Does that make sense?"

I'm nodding and already feel the heaviness lifting in my chest. She's right. I'm stronger now than I was back in high school. I'm every bit as good as the Carvers. I can fit in and handle this with flying colors. "Yes, it does. That helps."

"I'm only a phone call away if you need some moral support."

"Thanks for the advice and support, Talia."

"Always. Keep in touch and let me know how it goes."

"Will do. Have a good weekend."

Once I hang up with Talia, I slip my phone in my purse, then move all of "my stuff" to the trunk of Celeste's car before I get back in the car and head for Celeste's home.

As soon as I drive up the massive circular drive at the Carver estate, I'm immediately bombarded by Celeste's bodyguard, Marco. He's no more than six feet, but he's a brute of a man with dark wavy hair that he wears super short and a bullish face that says he's one red flag away from charging. "Where the hell have you been?" he snaps as he pulls my car door open.

Celeste had told me how she ditched him while he was off sneaking a smoke. The guy really is clueless that she knows how to use his habits to her own advantage. What she didn't warn me to expect is the way he addresses her.

"Excuse me?" I adopt an attitude I've seen Celeste use several times with guys at school who thought they could even *try* to talk to her. Climbing out of my car, I meet his angry gaze. "You'd better button it, Marco, or you'll find yourself out of a job."

He stiffens and puffs his chest up. "Your father is my employer, not you. You will never leave this estate again without me. Got it?"

I rage inside. In my mind I tell him where he can shove his self-important attitude, but the words lodge in my throat. Instead, I raise my eyebrows. "We'll see about that."

Turning, I walk away and head straight inside only pausing to speak to a tall woman wearing a black skirt and starched white blouse, her dark hair in a French twist. "Can you tell me where my father is, Beatrice?"

When she pauses to stare at me while arranging the tall flowers in a vase on the console near the library, a moment of panic squeezes my chest. *Does she realize I'm not Celeste?* I tell myself it's all in how confident you act, but the truth is... my anger at Marco is the only thing that's going to get me through this meeting with Gregory that Celeste insisted on. I keep my features composed, but my stomach is knotting tight. "I need to speak with him about something."

"He's in his office, Celeste. If you want, I'll knock and see if he's off the phone yet."

Exhaling my relief that I passed her scrutiny, I wave as I breeze past her. "That's not necessary. I'll just wait for him to finish."

Marco is right behind me, his shoes slapping the wood floor leading to Celeste's father's office. Just as I reach for the knob, he says quickly, "You can't just walk in there."

"Watch me," I say, clinging to my anger as I open the

door and step into the room with a confident attitude. I try my best to ignore my pounding heart and the absolute knee-knocking fear I'm about to get caught.

Celeste's father turns his leather chair away from the window, his silver head swiveling around to face us, his thick brows raised in question.

God, I can't believe I'm pretending to be his daughter. This is so fucked up!

I immediately take one of the cushioned seats in front of his desk. If I hadn't my legs might've just given out on me. When Marco sits in the chair next to me, his face reflecting an apologetic look toward Celeste's father, I straighten my spine and pin a patient smile on my face.

"I understand your position, Jonas. There's still a lot of work to be done in that area," Celeste's father says. "I can't really discuss the details at this time. I just wanted you to know we're working on it." He nods. "Yes, I'll see you tonight."

As soon as he hangs up, I open my mouth to speak, but he overrides me. "Celeste Ann Carver. You know better than to walk into my office while I'm on a business call."

Apparently Celeste's relationship with her father is far more formal than mine is with my dad. It didn't matter if he was on a business call negotiating the most important contract of the year, my father's eyes would light up the moment he saw my face. He'd silently beckon me in, then meet me halfway across the room to give me a hug. Yes, I'd be quiet and sit down to wait for him to finish, but this man's response is so alien to me, I just blink at him for a second before I can collect myself.

"I'm sorry, Father." The fact Celeste uses the formal term to address her dad should've clued me in. *Did my voice just shake?* Ugh, clearing my throat, I clench my hands together on my lap. "Marco claims that since *you're* his employer, he can talk to me any way he wants."

When the Senator instantly frowns at my bodyguard and demands, "Is this true?" I take a steadying breath.

"That-that's not what I said," Marco stutters, jerking upright to a more formal position in the chair.

I'm so relieved that I seemed to have passed her father's initial inspection that I answer as if *I* was the one Marco offended. "Did you *not* curse at me the moment I drove up?"

Marco's face reddens. "That's only because you took off without me."

"Celeste," Gregory warns, frowning at me. "That's entirely unacceptable. You know you're not to leave the house without your bodyguard."

Right now *I'm* totally on Celeste's side about canning this asshole. "What good does having a bodyguard do if he can't even tell that someone is following me?"

"No one is following you!" Marco raises his voice, clearly agitated as he pulls on his tie to loosen it. "And if that were really true, why would you take off without me?"

"To prove how easily I can, which means *you're* not doing your job," I say, refusing to back down from his resentful gaze.

Marco starts to speak when Gregory cuts in, "Enough!"

Pointing to Marco, he narrows his gaze. "Do your job, Marco. Now get the hell out!"

"But—" he cuts himself off at Gregory's hard stare, then glares at me before leaving.

Once the door shuts behind him, I say, "Thank you for—"

"Silence. We need to talk," the Senator barks.

Oh God...does he know I'm not Celeste? I'm shaking on the inside so hard, I curl my hands into fists beside my thighs.

Gregory scowls. "I have a lot on my plate right now. I don't have time to deal with petty stuff like this, Celeste. Stop playing games with Marco. You will wait for him to follow before you leave here. Not only is your safety at risk, but that of our family. I shouldn't have to remind you that the Carver business is in *your* name."

It is? What the hell? Celeste didn't mention it. I'm just so relieved he's calling me Celeste that I don't immediately respond. But that does makes sense that the Carver business would be in Celeste's name now. According to the info Celeste gave me on her family, her mother has lupus. She's too ill to take on much responsibility. They must've made the change of leadership of the family business to Celeste when her father accepted the Senate appointment. In his new role, he would need to avoid a conflict of interest with the private business sector.

"There is no one stalking you. No one is watching you. I refuse to have this discussion again, Celeste. Is that understood?" The finality in her father's tone draws me out of my thoughts.

Shocked by his seeming indifference for his daughter's wishes, I tilt my chin higher. If there's even a chance that Celeste is right and her bodyguard is a total idiot—the asshole part has already been established—then she needs to be protected by someone she trusts to have her back.

I reach for my earlier anger to get me through this. "Since I'm the head of Carver Enterprises, that means that technically I'm Marco's employer."

When the Senator's expression hardens, I hold up my hand. "Calder Blake is coming to the event today. You know his qualifications."

"I can't find anything on him since he left the military nine months ago, Celeste." Gregory pulls out a folder from a drawer, opening it on his desk. "Honestly, his Blake family connection has more appeal to me than his qualifications as a personal guard."

I mask my annoyance at how easily he brushes his daughter's concerns off. "Consider it a double win, then. When you meet him today, please listen to what he has to say. I think you'll be impressed by him."

The Senator snorts and adds to his wiry six-foot height, buttoning his suit jacket. "We shall see. For now let's table the subject. I need to leave for a meeting in five minutes."

After being summarily dismissed, I head upstairs. I text Celeste as I walk down the hall, heading for her room.

Your bodyguard is an ass.

I start to type "And so is your father" but then delete it. *Yes, he is.*

Smirking that we agree about Marco, I reply. *Would've been nice to know YOU'RE Carver Enterprises now.*

Don't let the title fool you.

I start to ask what she means by that, but I gasp as I nearly run into a pretty girl in her early twenties with delicate features, light brown hair and big green eyes.

"Sheesh, Celeste, I thought you'd given up social media."

Has she? Interesting. I quickly tuck the phone in my purse. "Hey, Lizzy. Are you looking forward to the cocktail?"

Celeste's younger sister blinks at me. "Beth! You know how much I hate Lizzy." She corrects me, rolling her eyes. "And is that a trick question? You know I'd rather be flayed alive."

Celeste knows Beth hates the name Lizzy. She uses it constantly to annoy her sister. Snickering, I continue on toward Celeste's room, calling back to her. "The torture begins in three hours. The bar's open at five. Don't be late."

"Don't worry. I know how to put on a show."

When I glance back, she's already gone from the hall. Ah, that's right...her room was the door I passed a second ago.

Celeste's bedroom is at the end of the hall. I knew it was massive based on the house layout she went over with me, but seeing the plush sofa seating area next to a marble fireplace against the far wall, a desk/library combo space on one side of the room, a massive king-sized sleigh bed on the other, and a full sized bathroom off the far left corner of the huge space really drills her family's wealth home. My entire apartment could fit in her bedroom. Correction—suite.

Leaning against the door, I take several deep breaths, glad to be away from scrutinizing eyes.

So far, so good.

*U*NBELIEVABLE! I mentally fuss as I watch the pearl earring I tried to put in my ear bounce against the bed before disappearing into the cream-colored carpet. Getting down on my hands and knees in the fitted velvet dress is a feat in itself, but after a minute of running my hand across the carpet under the bed and in front of the nightstand, I'm about to give up when I decide to run my fingers just under the nightstand itself.

"Gotcha," I mutter in triumph. As I start to straighten with the earring in my hand, I glance up and see a quarter-inch wide red ribbon poking out the underside of the nightstand. Once I put the earring in, I quickly pull the drawer open and furrow my brow. Other than a couple of books, some nail polish and some pens, there's nothing in the drawer with a ribbon on it.

I slide the drawer closed and peer under the nightstand once more, this time pushing on the underside. I'm surprised when the wood gives, then tilts with the weight of something sliding right before a gold-paged book falls onto the floor. I stare at the black book, it's red ribbon bookmark standing out against the light carpet.

"Are you kidding me?" I whisper, lifting the book and staring at the gold lock holding the diary closed. As unbelievable as it seems for someone who used to share a large part of her personal life on social media, what better place to keep secrets than off-line where no one can get to them? So long as no one knows it exists, I think as I push on the button to see if the lock will release. When it doesn't budge, I sigh. *Maybe this is a reminder you're not supposed to snoop.*

Then she shouldn't have given me full access to her room, I rationalize as I move to her desk and sift through the drawer. Once I find a paperclip, I unbend it and try my best to unlock the diary without scratching the gold lock.

After a few tries, I toss the paperclip in the trash and set the book down on the desk. Leaning on my hands, I stare at it, itching to know what someone like Celeste would write about. *Who stole her fashion idea? Her latest boyfriend? Who she screwed over in payback?*

As I lean forward, the necklace swings back and forth, blocking my view of the lock. The second I wrap my fingers around it to stop its movement, my gaze zeroes on the key. It looks about the right size. *What if...*

I quickly remove the necklace and slide the key into the lock, then let out a low triumphant laugh when the latch pops open.

Once I hook the necklace back around my neck, a twinge of guilt hits me as I open the book. When I see she has dated her entries that go all the way back to 1998, my conscience won't let me read it, but I can't help flipping to the day she played that prank on me. Yeah, I know the date. I'll never forget it. What was running through her head that day? *Did she plan it? Did she feel any remorse? Did I even rate a mention?*

SEPTEMBER 23, 2006

DOES she realize that I helped her?

I STARE AT THE PAGE, then flip to a couple entries before and after this one. In each of the other entries, she wrote long poetry type passages. Flipping back to the one entry on the twenty-third, I stare at the sentence. I know it's not about me, because there's no way what she did could ever be considered generous or helpful. Words like *spiteful* and *cruel* come to mind. Who was she talking about?

A knock at the door makes me jump. "Come on, Celeste. Dad's waiting on us," Beth calls through the heavy wood.

"Go on down. I'll just be a minute," I say as I quickly snap the lock closed and move to put the diary back where I found it.

I'm halfway down the hall, when my clutch purse vibrates in my hand. Pulling Celeste's phone out, I read her message.

Calder is supposed to arrive right around six. You'll need to greet him at the entrance, since he doesn't know anyone.

She must've really kept their dating on the down-low if no one in her family has met Calder yet. I quickly respond.

What time do you think you'll make it back tonight? I'm willing to meet you somewhere, so long as you tell me how to shake Marco.

Not sure yet. I'll let you know.

Damn, I hate the uncertainty of not knowing exactly when this charade will end.

I cross the huge entryway and enter the big room with a vaulted ceiling and glass doors across the entire curved wall on the other side of the room. I pause in the doorway when I catch sight of a thin, elegantly dressed dark-haired woman sitting in a chair and holding court with the few guests who have arrived early. The last thing I want to do is go near Nadine Carver.

If anyone can spot an imposter, it's the mother.

CHAPTER TWELVE

THE OBSERVER

I stand out of sight, staring at them talking politics and upcoming elections in the fall. Wealth rubbing shoulders with wealth, hoping even more wealth will rub off on them. What I *want* can't be bought. I deserve it, but it's not mine. Not yet, but soon.

I scan the room, seeking Celeste. My heart thumps when my gaze lands on her. She's talking to her younger sister. I study Elizabeth with an unbiased eye. She is pretty with the mischievous streak of someone who has never known suffering or sadness. She makes you smile and enjoy her company, but her eyes don't hold the depth that Celeste's do. She has more layers than I ever knew, making her even more interesting.

She is beautiful. Her smile is genuine, her eyes alight with curiosity at everyone around her. When Ben walks up and she calls him Batman, I tense. What the hell is that about?

I watch him touch her hand while he talks about his plans to set up his medical practice and my gaze slits. Fury clenches my insides. *You don't have permission to touch her. She's not yours. She'll never be yours. Celeste belongs to me.* Only me.

I skim my gaze over her face once more and shake off the anger at myself for not pushing my plans for Celeste forward before now.

She will resist like she always has. And a part of me will enjoy hurting her for all the suffering she's put me through. But the thought of making her bleed so that things will fall in line makes me smile.

She's held me off long enough. Soon, I'll own her body and soul.

CHAPTER THIRTEEN

CASS

I shake my head in bemusement as I watch Ben Hemming walk away to get a drink. He's just a year younger than Jake, but it's hard to believe he and Jake are related. It had been great to put a face with the nice guy in the Batman costume I danced briefly with at the masked party.

Even though I had to pretend I already knew who he was, Ben was easy to talk to. I remember him being on the thin side that night at the party, but in four years his hair had turned an even darker brown and he had filled out to a sleek, athletic build. Apparently he's whip smart to already have his medical degree a whole year sooner than his peers.

Unlike most of the types slowly filling up the Carver's ballroom, Ben didn't come across as the kind of person to dissect every word I uttered for its worth and credibility. Instead, he laughed at my quips about politics, saying, "You should be bluntly honest more often. It's charming, Celeste. You're making me reconsider." Our conversation had been pleasant, like normal people chatting at a party.

"Celeste, come and greet our guests." Nadine's green gaze spears past the businessmen in front of her and she waves, beckoning me forward.

My stomach tenses into knots as I approach Celeste's mother. How I manage a smile once I reach her side, I have no idea. She looks tired, but even with her illness she's still a very attractive woman. "You look beautiful," I say as I take her hand and admire her floor length black chiffon dress and the four-caret teardrop diamond pendant earrings that match her necklace.

Nadine's gaze holds mine long enough to make me squirm. When she finally squeezes my hand and smiles, her gaze sliding over the off-the-shoulder bodice and long, fitted sleeves, to the tea-length pencil-style skirt, I slowly exhale my pent up breath. Paired with Celeste's red-bottomed black patent pumps, the dress manages to be both elegant and subtly sexy. I'm just so glad the back forms a deep-vee to my waist. It might've made wearing the bra Celeste bought for it impossible to wear, but at least then I won't get over-heated. Apparently fitted velvet is quite warm.

"That wine color is exquisite on you, dear," Nadine says before turning to the two men she'd been speaking to. "Gentlemen, my oldest daughter, Celeste." Looking at me, she indicates the thin-faced, middle-aged man with rosy cheeks. "You remember Governor Marlin."

As the Governor shakes my hand, the blond-haired man to his right smiles at me. "I'm Alan Warren, Celeste."

I welcome the Governor, then turn to Mr. Warren. "It's nice to meet you, Mayor Warren."

Clearly pleased to be recognized, Alan takes my hand once the Governor releases it. "It's wonderful to meet you. I hope you'll come as our special guest at the upcoming city-council meeting next week?"

A moment of panic grips me, seizing my throat. I manage to smile and make a *mhmm* sound. The mayor is in his early forties with honest brown eyes and the firm hand-shake of someone who stands by what he says. I hope politics doesn't ruin that about him.

I release his hand and realize too late that the way he's grinning at me means I must've just agreed. Well crap. So much for no one asking me tough questions.

"I'm sure, Celeste will make every effort to be there, Alan, but her schedule is pretty full with family business duties."

As the mayor nods his understanding, I slide an appreciative look Nadine's way. I have no clue what Celeste really does if her title in the family business is just that, but I can't help but be a bit in awe of Celeste's mother. This whole way of life is so alien to me, yet despite her illness Nadine maneuvers through the murkiness like an elegant swan gliding across a pond. Watching Alan take it in stride, clearly enthralled by her charms makes me realize just how one-dimensional photography can be. I can't possibly capture *all* the nuances that go on underneath the glitz and glamour.

A tall, well-built man in his early-fifties walks up to our group. "Good evening, gentlemen. You look as lovely as ever, Nadine," he says as he offers her his hand.

Nadine folds his between hers and gives him a warm smile. "Thank you for coming, Phillip. You know how much Gregory appreciates all the support you give our family."

Laying his free hand over hers, his smile is magnetic. "Your husband is going places and I plan to be right there with him."

Phillip Hemming.

I quickly glance around the crowded room and blow out a thankful breath. Jake doesn't appear to be here. Until Celeste briefed me, I had no idea that she knew Jake outside of school. Jake's father has been Carver Enterprises legal counsel for well over a decade. Phillip has also been Gregory's close friend and confidant for almost twenty years. I got the impression their families had gone on some vacations together when the kids were younger, so Celeste must see Jake and Ben like quasi-brothers. Maybe that's why she refused to date Jake. Then again, it could be she just didn't have any interest in him.

I glance around and finally spot Phillip's dark-haired, tan, and perfectly botox-ed wife, Lana, chatting up a storm with the wives near the bar.

I try not to look too closely at Phillip as he talks to Celeste's mother, but with his blond hair turning a bit lighter at his temples, I can definitely see where Jake got his striking good looks. Ben is pleasant looking, and he favors his mother's coloring, but Jake got his father's light hair, hazel eyes, and raw appeal. Unfortunately, I know how deceiving a handsome face can be. It might be unfair of me to make the father guilty by handsome-association, but I really don't want to be around him. As I look for an opportunity to gracefully slip away, I start to step back, but Phillip turns to me, his forehead pinched. "You look a little flushed, Celeste. Maybe you should get some water."

I lift my glass of soda. "I've got a drink, thanks."

Phillip starts to say something else, but then Beth's voice sounds behind me. "Look who I found, Celeste?"

When I turn, I'm unprepared to see Calder standing next to Celeste's sister.

Wearing a black suit and a slight smile, he looks like he could easily be one of the fashion models I book for my shoots. His hair is a bit longer than the last time I saw him, but still short by most guy's standards. And damn if I hadn't been right about his bone structure. The past several years have bulked out his broad shoulders and honed his striking features. I can't believe how devastatingly handsome he's become. With high cheekbones and an angular jaw, he's absolutely breathtaking. But his eyes hold a wariness I don't remember seeing before. It makes him both beautiful and even more unattainable at the same time.

"Well then." Beth's gaze pinging between us makes me realize I haven't said a single word. "I'm heading to the bar. Anyone want a drink?"

While Nadine asks Beth to bring her a glass of wine, I'm

so mesmerized by the fact Calder's green eyes are a couple shades darker than I remember, all I can do is blurt out, "You're here."

He nods, a smirk teasing his lips. "I am."

I want so badly to throw my arms around his neck and beg his forgiveness. No, first I want to kiss his sexy mouth and make him feel as loopy as I do while staring at him, and then beg his forgiveness.

I tilt my head and smile. "And you're early."

His smile fades. "I see you're astute as always."

I'm so stunned by the sudden shift in his demeanor, that it takes me a second to realize Nadine is speaking. "Celeste, don't be rude. Introduce your guest."

"Oh, sorry." I hook my hand on Calder's forearm and turn him toward the group. As introductions are made and he pulls free of my hold to shake hands, I watch him. He chats with the men and Nadine about local politics so easily you'd think he was born to it. No wonder he and Celeste hit it off. The realization that Celeste wasn't exaggerating about their ability to connect hits me hard, churning my stomach.

After Beth hands her mother a glass of wine, she pulls me back from the group and whispers, "How have you kept your hands off that handsome specimen? There's no way Scrappy knows about him or I'd have heard about it. Speaking of which..." Trailing off, she looks around. "Where is he?"

Who the heck is Scrappy? I shrug and hate that I can't think of a way to ask without making Beth suspicious. "Have you seen Father anywhere?"

Beth nods toward the French doors. "He stepped out there to answer a call."

"At his own party? Are you kidding me? I'll go get him. Tell Calder I'll be right back."

She gives me a funny look. "Brave girl. You're acting so odd."

Damn, apparently I'm being too me *right now.* May as well own it. I shrug. "Sometimes rocking the boat doesn't do the trick; you have to turn the dang thing over."

"Ooh, I like this feisty side of you," Beth calls after me, chuckling.

Cigar smoke is the only thing that greets me when I walk outside. Celeste mentioned that her father likes to occasionally smoke cigars, so I follow the scent across the patio and down the lantern-lit stairs.

The smell fades once I reach the garden, a seven-foot hedge maze with ground lights spearing up from under the tall bushes every few feet. Though it's not fully dark yet, the lights add a nice touch. A fountain gurgles in the center of the maze, and farther out, the scent of pine blows in the light wind from the evergreens lining the back of the property. As I make my way through the maze, I notice a few patches of white and yellow daffodils trying to pop through.

Knowing the future of my father's business is riding on my success tonight is weighing down every move I take in there. It feels good to take a breather away from the crowd. Celeste asked me to make sure that Calder is intro-duced to her dad, so I keep moving toward the center of the maze. The open space in the middle of the maze is empty except for a tall stone fountain and four wrought iron benches facing each other along the edge of the hedges.

I'm frustrated that I didn't find Gregory, but before I head back inside, I look up at the full moon already visible in the dusky sky. Purple and pink streak the quickly darkening skyline as the sun sets. I inhale the soothing scent of fresh outdoors and welcome the cool nip in the spring air, hoping both will reinforce my confidence that I can pull the rest of this evening off.

When someone touches the exposed skin on my right shoulder, true fear jumps to my throat. *Was Celeste right about a stalker?* I gasp and try to jerk away, but my attacker clamps a firm hand on my shoulder and steps behind me. I try to pry his hand loose, but the man's hold only tightens, locking me in place.

"Calm down. It's just me."

Calder's voice instantly halts my flight, but not my thudding heart. It races even more as I let go of his fingers. "You scared the crap out of me." I can't really turn with him holding me in place, so I press my hand to my chest and inhale through my nose, trying to calm myself down.

"You're safe," he says in an even tone. "I have questions."

"My father can answer—"

"But right now I want to know one thing..." Moving closer, his voice's deep timbre rumbles against my back.

While my heart thumps double-time, the warm sensation of his thumb sliding along my exposed skin brings tears of regret to my eyes. I quickly blink them away. "What?" I ask, trying hard not to let him hear the tension in my voice.

Easing back, he runs two fingers from my shoulder to my spine. Trailing his fingers down the center of my back, he says in a low tone, "Do you still want what's between us?"

I wish he were asking *me* that and not Celeste. Celeste sounded like she couldn't keep her hands off him, but I want so much more. I don't even know how to begin to answer his question.

His fingers slow to a sensual crawl along my skin. "I want the truth. I can't take another fucking lie in my life right now."

What is he talking about? What has he been doing since he got back to New York? My own questions derail when he reaches the bottom of the vee at my lower back.

Leaning close, his lips touch my ear. "Are the chill bumps from me touching you or because you're cold?"

My stomach tumbles and my legs feel like they'll stop holding me up at any moment. I swallow and answer honestly. "I'm not cold, Calder."

Calder touches my zipper, then presses a kiss to my shoulder right where he bit me that night. "Will you let me touch you?"

My insides tighten. "You aren't already?"

He slides his fingers down the left side of my neck, then shifts them forward to rest against the hollow of my throat. Massaging along the back of my neck with his thumb, his voice hardens. "Not in the way I want to."

Is he doing some kind of sexy role-playing with Celeste?

He never asked permission to touch me that night. He assumed...no, he demanded that I give us a chance.

"Answer me," he orders, sounding so much more like the Calder I remember. When his fingers flex against my throat, my body instantly responds to the edgy tension in his hold. The gruff command in his voice chips away at my resolve to keep my distance.

But he's not yours, Cass. He's Celeste's. I chant this over and over in my head as he traces his lips down the side of my neck. When he slips a hand inside the open back of my dress and folds his fingers possessively around my ribcage, my brain stutters. All I can focus on is the intense desire making me throb so hard my stomach knots.

"I'm waiting."

Hearing his seductive deep baritone rips a hole in my heart. I want to feel him touching me like that again so much. But this is wrong. He thinks he's with Celeste. *I'm the person he wants, damn it!* Or I was. My emotions swing wildly, making it hard to think of the right response.

"One thing you'd better learn about me, angel. Don't hesitate." Before I can say anything, he yanks down on my zipper and then slides his hands inside my dress and up along my ribcage. But instead of instantly clasping my breasts the way I expect him too, he barely touches the flat of his palms to the tips of my nipples. "Hesitation makes me think you aren't sure about us."

He says the last with such a cold tone, I start to tell him he couldn't be more wrong, but then he begins to move his palms in a slow sensuous circle along my nipples. Teasing, torturing...tantalizing. Brushing his lips against my earlobe, his voice amps up the enticing current running over my skin. "Have you ever been turned inside out with want?"

Only once. Tightness pulls at my core with each rotation his hands make. The slight drag and brush against me is putting my nerves on high alert. I swallow back a moan and counter his question. "Have *you?*"

His knowing chuckle vibrates along my nerve endings. The sensation rushes through my body, igniting prickly heat where his palms connect with my nipples. "I'm going to own every breath you take. Every gasp and moan. Every shudder you experience will come from me."

The combination of his sexy promise heating me from the inside, while cool air blows across my skin is so arousing, I bite my lip to keep from whimpering. I know I should, but I don't stop him from pressing fully against my back. I can't decide what excites me more: his confidence that he can actually control my responses, or the fact I want him to be incredibly freaking successful. Then again, he probably always got Celeste off without much effort. That sudden thought sends a jolt of jealousy shooting through me, yanking me back to reality.

Damn, he's got me so caught up, I'm freaking panting and trying to lean into his hands. I know I'm only deluding myself with wishful imaginings about us.

I take a breath and tuck all my rioting emotions back behind the persona I'm supposed to be playing tonight—the platonic host. As I try to detach my emotions, I feel twitchy and ready to snap, like a live wire forced to ground itself. I don't like that he didn't answer my question, nor do I like that he's acting completely unaffected. But that's probably for the best.

"No one owns my responses but me," I say at the same time I start to push his hands away from my breasts.

Before I can connect, Calder grips my breasts in a tight, dominant hold and hauls me fully against him, rasping against my neck, "Am I going to have to fuck you right here in the middle of this garden just to prove you wrong?"

Yes! While my mind screams for me to answer him, I press my lips together, but I don't seem to have control over the rest of my body. My fingers slide into his thick hair and crush the soft strands. Tugging hard, I pull him close.

"Celeste, are you out here?" a man's voice sounds from somewhere close inside the maze.

Once Calder quickly zips my dress back up, I call out lightly, "I'm in the center by the fountain."

A few seconds later Phillip emerges from the maze. "There you are." He doesn't even glance at Calder as he continues, "Your father asked me to find you since he had to take your mother up to her room. He'll be making an announcement soon."

"I came out here looking for Father so he could meet Calder."

Phillip sizes Calder up with one look. "So...a Blake working as a bodyguard. I'm sure your family is thrilled."

I glare at Phillip. "That was unnecessary—"

"I haven't made any decisions in that regard," Calder cuts in, his voice tight. "I came tonight as Celeste's guest."

"The Carvers have been well-guarded for years." Phillip says dismissively to Calder, but then turns his hazel gaze my way. "I don't see the point of disrupting a security team that works."

"Celeste's security guard was smoking outside when I came in. In doing so, he's leaving his charge vulnerable. That puts the Carvers at risk. Even those close to them could become collateral damage." Calder holds a steady gaze on Phillip. "Like you."

Annoyance flashes in Phillip's eyes before he clears his throat. "The last thing Gregory needs right now is change. Any kind of change." He turns to me. "You need to consider *that* with your request, Celeste. Exposing your family to strangers who aren't familiar with the dynamics could bring more harm than good. I'll speak to your father about Marco's smoke breaks."

I straighten to my full height. "I'm perfectly capable of addressing my own issues with my father, Phillip. Now if you'll excuse us, we should get back so I can introduce Calder."

We start to walk away when Phillip says, "Beth is waiting to introduce you to Gregory, Mr. Blake. Celeste will join you in a minute. I need to discuss some Carver business with her."

Panic grips me. I know nothing about Carver Enterprises. I wave him off. "It's a party. This can wait until tomorrow." *When Celeste is here to deal with you overbearing jerks.* Who knew her life was controlled so heavily. In high school *she* came across as the controlling one.

"No, it can't, Celeste. This matter needs your attention now."

Trying not to look annoyed, I smile at Calder. "Go on. I'll join you and my father in just a minute."

A muscle jumps in his jaw as he glances at Phillip. "Are you sure?"

I nod. "I'll be right behind you."

Phillip doesn't speak until he hears Calder enter the house. "What the hell are you doing out here with him? You should be inside working to gain more supporters."

His tone completely shifts from concerned business colleague and family friend to authoritarian. I'm so shocked by the change I just stare at him. "I thought you wanted to discuss Carver business."

His face darkens. "This *is* business. Your father has no plans to hire him. I know that for a fact, so get the idea out of your head and don't bring him around here any more."

I jerk my chin up, my gaze challenging him. "I will invite whomever I want to my own home, Phillip. You're way overstepping."

"*I'm* overstepping?" The irritation in his expression shifts, then he jerks his chin toward the house, a knowing smirk tilting his lips. "He doesn't know, does he?"

"Doesn't know what?" I snap, narrowing my gaze.

When Phillip lets out a low laugh, I roll my eyes and start to leave, but he grabs my arm in a tight hold and pulls me back to face him, his tone turning cold. "You belong to the Carver dynasty, Celeste. Don't go getting any other ideas. Your father will be making an announcement in five minutes. Get in there and show your respect and support."

He talks like the Carver name is a living, breathing entity that he has a vested interest in. Then again, maybe he's a business partner too. Regardless, none of that gives him a right to talk to Celeste like he is. I breathe in and out of my nose a couple of times to rein my temper in. "Let go of me," I grit out and jerk free of his hold.

He stares at me as if surprised that I dared to challenge him. Before I say something Celeste might have to pay for later, I turn and walk away.

What was that all about? There are some major undercurrents going on here that Celeste didn't clue me in on. I want so badly to text her about Phillip's bossy behavior—he lords authority over her more than her own father does—but I can't take the time. I need to be in there with her father and Calder. I promised I would try to help smooth the way.

When I walk in, I pause at the sight of Jake by the bar. With a drink in hand, he catches my eye and smiles. Before he can walk in my direction, I shake off the sudden tension and shift my gaze away, heading straight for Celeste's father and Calder talking on the other side of the room.

I reach Calder's side just as Gregory says, "SEAL training isn't the same as being in personal security, Mr. Blake. You'll be following her shopping, eating out, and going to clubs." Celeste's father highlights the frivolous parts of Celeste's life as he cuts his gaze to me. "But for whatever reason my daughter has gotten it in her head that you'll make a better bodyguard than Marco."

Marco, who's standing fifteen feet away in the corner of the room, perks up upon hearing his name. When he narrows his gaze on me, I barely resist the urge to flip him off. *Asshole.*

Calder folds his hands behind his back and nods. "I haven't agreed to take on the role, but for Celeste's sake, I've done a cursory evaluation and have already discovered ways that your daughter's security can be improved."

"Excellent!" Gregory claps Calder on the shoulder, smiling. "Please convey these to Marco. You'll be paid well for your consulting services, Mr. Blake."

My mouth drops open. "Could you *be* any more insulting?"

Calder glances my way, his expression impassive. "Your father doesn't share your views on necessary personnel changes to improve security."

"That's not what I said," Gregory blusters. "Of course my daughter's safety is incredibly important, but so is a team that works like a well-oiled machine. I don't want to dismantle that."

I'm so frustrated and angry it's hard to maintain an even tone. "Even if it means better security overall? This makes no sense to me."

Gregory looks at his watch, then puts his hand on my shoulder and squeezes lightly. "We'll discuss it later, Celeste. For now I need you to come with me. People are waiting."

Somewhat appeased that he said he'll discuss it further, I cast an apologetic gaze to Calder and follow Celeste's dad.

My steps slow as we approach the Hemming family standing in the entryway. I instantly look at Beth next to Jake and Ben and then the guys' parents.

Just as I raise my eyebrows in a "what's going on" question at Beth, she moves to give us space. Gregory falls in line beside Beth. When he turns to face the room, I slide into line next to Ben. *Why didn't Celeste mention this part of the event?* With anxious anticipation knotting my stomach, I keep my gaze on Celeste's dad while Phillip raises his voice above the crowd.

"Can we have everyone's attention please? Gregory has an important announcement to make."

Celeste's father raises his hands to get the people to settle down. Once everyone turns to face us, Gregory says, "As you know, I invited you here to garner your support for my campaign, but there's also another reason our friends and colleagues are gathered here tonight. "I'm pleased to announce the merger of the Carvers and the Hemmings families through my daughter's engagement to Phillip's son."

I turn wide eyes to Beth, shocked that she didn't mention she was getting engaged. When she gives me a "what?" look, I shift my gaze away. It's bad enough that she just saw surprise on my face; If it's Jake, I don't want her to see the worried concern reflected in my eyes.

Gregory is droning on, happily soaking up the moment. "Phillip and I have been neighbors and close friends for nineteen years, and we couldn't be happier that our children are going to marry and officially make us a true family. Congratulations to Ben and Celeste!"

As I jerk my attention to Gregory's face, Ben slips his hand around mine. Folding our fingers together, he whispers in my ear to be heard over the hoots of congratulations and clapping. "Mrs. Ben Hemming. How does that sound? I promise to give you a massive diamond tomorrow. My dad was adamant we announce it today."

It's so hard not to immediately jerk my hand free. Ben seems like a nice guy, but this is the strangest engagement announcement. *Why didn't he say something to me about it earlier? He didn't even hint at it. And why didn't Celeste warn me?*

All I want to do is bolt, but I can't. This is a freaking nightmare. The idea of being Jake's sister-in-law, even a fake one for an evening, is too much for me. As nausea quickens in my belly, I force a smile as the ladies approach to congratulate us. The moment they walk away, I stiffen when Jake moves behind us and throws his arms over Ben and my shoulders.

"Well, isn't this just nice and cozy? I didn't think you had the balls, bro."

The blatant anger and sarcasm in his voice is only for our ears, but I don't miss the wince in Ben's expression when his brother tightens his arm hold on his neck. I don't want Jake touching me at all. Resisting the urge to punch him where it counts, I jam my elbow in his rib and say lightly, "Nice and tactful, Jake." The only reason I'm able to keep a pleasant look on my face is because Jake's obviously pissed.

I'm still going to kill Celeste for not warning me about

this. But as much as Jake leaning close and whispering in my ear, "You have no idea just how nasty I can be, Celeste," freaks me out, my mind fixates on the most important question to come from this announcement—what the hell was Celeste doing messing around with Calder if she knew she was getting engaged to Ben?

Calder!

My gaze shifts to where I left him before I had to walk to the front of the room. He's not there. I murmur my thanks to the few more people who approach to offer congrats to Ben and me, while furtively scanning the room for Calder's broad shoulders. I can't find him anywhere. He probably left. I don't blame him; I wouldn't stick around. I clench my hand into a fist knowing today was probably the last time I'll ever see him.

My stomach twists with so much fury and regret that I shove Jake's arm off my shoulder without a second thought as to who might see.

Shrugging free of his brother's hold, Ben glares at Jake and reaches for my hand once more. "Ignore whatever he said."

"She knows she picked the wrong brother," Jake sneers in a smug tone.

"I—I need to go to the bathroom." I pull from Ben's grasp and quickly walk toward the foyer, heading straight for the bathroom.

What kind of person invites the man she's sleeping with to her house to watch her get engaged to another guy? Did

Calder know he was just a friend-with-benefits? What twisted mind-fuck trip is Celeste on?

I pull the phone Celeste gave me out of my purse, and my hands shake as I fumble through typing a text.

I just got blindsided with an engagement announcement. It's bad enough that I'm having to pretend not to be shocked by this, but how the hell could you do that to Calder? Call me immediately or I'm going to walk back in there and blow your precious cover.

CHAPTER FOURTEEN

CASS

"Y ou can't tell them, Cass! Please. I promise that I didn't know they were going to announce the engagement tonight."

I lock the bathroom door behind me. Holding the phone tight, I rock my jaw back and forth so I don't scream at her. "Yet you think it's okay to lead Calder on like that? What happened to, 'he was the best thing that ever happened to you lately'?"

"He was...is. My marriage will be in name only. It's just a business arrangement. Nothing more."

"Did you tell Calder that?" I say in a tight voice.

A pause. "Not yet."

"Well, that's a damned shitty way for him to find out."

"I feel terrible about that. I'll apologize to him as soon as I get back."

"Give me his number. I'll do it." I need to do *something*.

"No, this is my fault. I will go see him and apologize in person."

"I doubt that'll do much good," I snap, feeling personally guilty for how much today had to have hurt him, especially after what happened between us in the garden. My emotions are so fucking wrapped up in Celeste's drama...to the point I've only made things worse. I should be glad that Calder probably despises Celeste now. And thrilled that he left without saying a word, but all I can think about is how he just got hammered with one of the worst lies ever. Betrayal.

"All I can do is try, Cass."

At least she sounds regretful and upset. I expel a frustrated sigh. "Your fiancé seems pretty happy right now." As soon as I say that, it occurs to me that Ben did hint at his interest. He'd said, "You're making me reconsider." *Shit, and here I thought he was talking about which political party he was supporting.* "I don't think Ben sees this marriage arrangement the way you do, Celeste."

"Wait...Ben?"

My stomach bottoms out at the surprise in her voice. "You were supposed to marry Jake?"

"Well, yeah...I mean, he's liked me since we were teens. I always assumed it would be Jake," she says slowly, then heaves a sigh. "I didn't mention it, because I didn't expect Jake to be there tonight. He hates politics."

I can't believe anyone would consider a sham marriage in modern times, but I'm almost done with this craziness, so what do I care. The fact that Ben is a part of this drops my opinion of him considerably. "What time are you getting back? I don't think I can deal with the controlling men around here much longer. I quietly told Phillip off earlier, but I came so close to loudly cursing him out."

"What did he say to you?" Celeste asks, her voice suddenly tense.

"Nothing. He just tried to shut down Calder becoming your bodyguard. He was worse about it than your father. What the heck is going on with him?"

"Phillip has his own agenda," she says quietly, then perks up. "Did you really tell him off?"

"I told him to mind his own business and that I can take care of my own."

Celeste giggles as if she can't stop herself. "That's fantastic. I'm sure he was pissed."

I shrug, then remember she can't see me. "I don't care. By the way, I tried, but your father nixed the idea for Calder as your bodyguard."

"I'm not surprised," Celeste grumbles.

"Okay, so back to me getting *back* to my own life. When can I meet you to hand off your car? I don't think my nerves can take much more."

"I just now got here. I'm the last appointment of the day and they've stayed open late for me. Honestly, I probably won't be back until around midnight, so I need you to continue to be me until then."

"Midnight?" I hiss quietly into the phone. *Where did she go? Timbuktu?* "I can't stay here another minute. I guess I can just leave after the cocktail is over and drive around until you call me."

"No, I need you to keep being me, Cass. That means you'll need to continue to be present and seen with my family. I'll text you where to meet me once I get back to town."

"But Ben—"

"I doubt Ben will try anything tonight—he's never tried with me. Hmmm, maybe he wants his dad to bankroll his practice. Anyway, if he does try to get affectionate, just claim a horrible headache and escape to my room."

"I thought I had to be *seen*," I say, unable to keep the annoyance out of my comment.

"You will be. Trust me. Beth will know if you're there or not. So please say you'll stay a bit longer. I just need to make it through tonight."

"Fine," I say on a sigh, telling myself that I'm almost done.

"See you later," she says before promptly hanging up.

As soon as I end the call, I hear deep voices in the foyer. I turn off the light in the bathroom and crack the door.

Jake is standing there talking to his father. He's obviously angry by the way he's gesturing. "You know I've always wanted her—"

His father rumbles.

"Bullshit, Dad—"

Phillips says something harsh in a low tone I can't make out.

Jake lowers his voice, but then he gets angry again and I catch the tail end of it. "—lied to me!"

Phillip gets in his son's face, his own red with anger. I strain to hear and just catch his last few words. "—riding on this."

"I'll going to kill that little prick," Jake grits out.

"Never threaten family, Jake," Phillip snaps in an angry tone, then narrows his gaze. "Don't you have somewhere to be?"

"Fuck this shit! I'm out of here."

When Jake leaves, I quietly close the door. I can only assume they were talking about Celeste and Ben's engagement. There was definitely a battle of wills going on.

After a full minute, I leave the bathroom, but then pause when I step into the empty foyer. Phillip is leaning against the wall near the entryway, his arms crossed as if waiting.

He watches me move my keys out of the way as I slip my phone into my small clutch. Lifting his eyes back to my face, his gaze narrows to slits. "Don't even think about it. You're going back in there and putting on a happy face the rest of the night."

I drop my keys beside my phone and snap my purse closed with a decisive click. He must think I planned to leave. I hold his gaze with a steady one. "I'll do what I please, Phillip. Stop trying to order me around." As I start to pass him, I call lightly over my shoulder, "Otherwise, I might just become your worst nightmare."

His scotch-warmed breath brushes next to my ear, his words a harsh grate. "I'll do whatever it takes to protect what's mine, Celeste. Don't force me to show you how ruthless I can be."

Even though the room is warm, a chill of worry slides through me, prickling my skin. I pick up my pace and move as far away from Phillip as fast as I can.

I don't see Beth in the main room, so I head straight for Ben. It's ironic that he's the only person I feel comfortable speaking with, but it's the truth. The moment I reach his side, he clasps my shoulders, his gaze concerned. "Are you okay?"

I nod and rub my forehead. "My head is killing me. If it's okay with you, I'm going to go upstairs and lie down."

"Do you want me to walk you up?"

I shake my head. "No, I'll be fine. You stay down here and be my proxy host."

When he smiles at my comment, I can't help but wonder why he's chosen a marriage of convenience. "Why would you lock yourself in like this, Ben?"

He releases me to push a strand of hair back from my face. "Because you're fun when you let yourself go." Running his finger down the side of my face, he continues, "And because you need a buffer so you can continue to do so."

Ben's sentiment is so sweet, my eyes mist. Celeste's life freaking sucks, but at least she'll have Ben's support. I can tell by the way he's looking at me that he's in love with her. I hope she treats him with equal respect and kindness.

But just in case she doesn't, he'll at least hear it from me.

Leaning close, I press a light kiss on his jaw and whisper in his ear, "Thank you for being a true knight."

When I leave the main room, I'm annoyed that Marco appears to be following me. *Now* he's going to do his job? *Screw that.* "You can stay down here," I say curtly, waving him off.

He shakes his head. "I need to follow you up."

"Since when?"

When he doesn't answer, I clench my jaw and walk upstairs, my shadow trailing behind me.

The second I walk into Celeste's bedroom, a true headache pounds behind my eyes. Locking the door, I immediately change out of the dress and heels. I can't get her stuff off fast enough, but once I'm naked, I don't have a choice, I have to choose something else to put on, so I dig through her closet past all the preppy stuff with patterns and bright colors until I find a lavender long-sleeved button down, a faded blue jean skirt and soft black leather ankle boots.

The outfit is as far from Celeste's normal wardrobe as I can get and more like me. I feel so much better once I'm dressed.

I take off her bracelets and the pearl earrings. Then I remove her necklace, but when I start to set it down on her dresser the key catches my attention.

I hesitate one second before I turn toward her night-stand and take out the diary.

Sitting on her bed, I flip to the very beginning. At first Celeste's entries are sparse.

September 7, 1998

I got a pony today! I guess I'd better learn how to ride.

July 4, 1999

Best 4th of July fireworks EVER! We went to the beach with the Hemmings. Jake won't stop pulling my hair. Ugh!

November 29, 1999

The Hemmings came to our Thanksgiving dinner. Ben is quiet. Jake is such a boy!

April 3, 2002

Mom got very sick and had to go to the hospital last week. She's home now but says she has lupus, which basically means she can get weak very easily. I don't want anything to happen to her.

January 2003

School. Friends. Shopping. Boys! Yeah, I suck at keeping up with this.

November 12, 2003

Mom is spending more time in her room. Between school-work, cheering practice, and games I'm lucky if I see her once a week. I miss her. Lizzy has decided she wants to be called Beth. I'll always think of her as Little Lizzy. (LL for short).

July 3, 2004

We're supposed to spend 4th of July week with the Hemmings at their vacation home.

July 4 – 11, 2005

I stare at the blank page and wonder why she bothered to start an entry but never filled it in. When I turn the page, the next entry is dated a whole year later, but that's when Celeste's writing turns into long poetic prose, full of metaphors talking about safe hidden passages, masks of happy faces, green greed and black deception. It's the kind of angst-y, self-introspection that seems far deeper than the Celeste I know...and yet only she can understand its meaning. Curious, I thumb forward through monthly entries now, and the poetic pattern continues. She only breaks it once, which is the entry I looked up earlier, September 23, 2006, where she wrote: *Does she realize that I helped her?*

I flip to the current year and read through several months. Same angst-y, introspective writing. She seems so... alone. I keep reading, trying to understand.

When a yawn overtakes me, I lean back on her pillow and close my eyes. A couple minutes won't hurt and might help my head. Just when I'm on the verge of falling asleep and in that zoned-out-almost-asleep state, I hear knocking and a man call Celeste's name. Grunting, I ignore it and roll over.

I jerk awake and groggily glance at the clock in surprise. I'd slept for two hours. At least I'm that much closer to freedom. Sighing, I pick up Celeste's diary wondering if she'd said anything about the switch we made. Just as I turn to the last page, a knock sounds on my door and Beth calls, "Celeste...did you get my text?" The doorknob turns but the lock holds. "Let me in."

"Just a minute." I grab the phone from my purse and take a picture of the last entry, then email it to myself to read later. For some reason I can't fathom, I want to understand what prompted Celeste to allow the one person she knew despised her into the most intimate part of her life.

Once I put the diary back in its hiding spot, I scroll through the most recent text from Beth to catch up with what I missed. It's the first time Celeste replied to someone else as herself. Or is it?

Out of curiosity, I look under the deleted texts to see what else I might've missed before she cleared it from the trash folder. The last thing I expect to see is a text conversation from a couple hours ago, right after I left the party. It's between Celeste and someone she has listed in her phone only as *Deceiver*. The name alone raises my eyebrows, but the tone of the texts alarms me more.

C: I'm done letting you control me. I'm taking care of it.

Deceiver: Don't threaten my legacy. Every part of you, inside and out, belongs to me.

C: Not any more.

Deceiver: We'll discuss this later.

C: You can't stop me.

A half hour passes between texts.

Deceiver: When did you leave? Where the fuck are you? You don't want to find out how ugly I can be.

C: I'd rather die than let you touch me EVER again.

Deceiver: You're very brave behind these texts. When I find you, you'll change your tune.

C: I hate the person I became because of you, you sick perverted bastard!

"Celeste!" Beth rattles the door handle.

Frustrated with Beth's impatience, I quickly copy the entire text conversation and email it to myself to read over again later, then delete the sent mail and the photo I'd taken from the trash folder. Celeste was probably too upset to realize she hadn't permanently deleted the texts, but she might remember and fix her error before I have a chance to read the rest. *Who was Celeste talking to?* By the tone, it's obviously a man. Of course my mind immediately flips through the men in her life: Her father, Marco, Phillip, Jake, Ben, and Calder.

"Celeste?"

"Just a sec," I call out and flip to the beginning of the text conversation Celeste had with her sister, apparently between her texts with the mystery guy.

Beth: Party obligation is over. All guests are now gone. Before you become an old married woman, go out with me tonight. Come see me in an hour and a half.

C: Where are we going?

Beth: I'll tell you once we get there. Come to my room the back way.

C: Okay

Right after that text is one from Celeste to me.

C: Beth wants you to go out with her. I know I told you to stay there, but you should go. You'll still be with a Carver. Just enjoy getting out of the fishbowl.

As much as I want to ask her about the other text conversation I wasn't supposed to see, I text Celeste back.

Text me when you get into town.

"Celeste!" Followed by a set of three knocks in a row.

Ugh. I open my door and snort at Beth. "Impatient much. I was changing clothes."

"You took long enough," Beth says, breezing into my

room. Once she shuts my door, she nods toward the bath-room and lowers her voice to a whisper. "Marco's still out there. We'll have to go this way. I don't want to miss the beginning. It's always the best part."

I slip my phone, the ID and a bit of cash from Celeste's wallet into my front pocket, then follow her into the bath-room. When she opens the linen closet door, I keep my face perfectly schooled as she pushes on the back wall. Once the panel slides out of the way, revealing a hidden crawl space between the walls, I realize this must be the "back way" mentioned in that text. Celeste didn't mention this secret passageway existed. Then again, I'm sure she didn't think I would have a need to use it.

I follow Beth along the narrow space she's lighting up with her cell phone. "The beginning of what?" I ask as I swat at a cobweb brushing against my hair.

She glances my way right when a shiver rolls through me and chuckles. "Better put your tough face on, Celeste. This place isn't for sissies."

I narrow my gaze. "Where the heck are you taking me?"

"You'll see."

I should be wary of her cheeky grin, but the unknown actually sounded better than staying in this fishbowl.

CHAPTER FIFTEEN

THE OBSERVER

*M*y fingers are numb with my tight grip on the steering wheel. I roll my head from one shoulder to the other, trying to ease the tension vibrating inside me as I speed along the dark highway. Celeste is drowning in her obligations. *I decide what she must and mustn't do, and who she truly belongs to.* I push on the gas pedal, picking up speed.

Car lights flash, nearly blinding me. As the vehicle zooms past, I look up and smile when the lights shine on her. She's right in front of me, waiting for me to fully claim her.

I slam the pedal to the floor, pushing toward my goal. The day has finally come for her to accept who's in charge.

This is your day of reckoning, Celeste.

CHAPTER SIXTEEN

CASS

"*S*o what was the deal with you and Calder?" Beth asks once we manage to ditch her security guy. Anthony is far better than Marco. He must know Beth pretty well because he was right on our tail as soon as we left the house. I thought for sure we wouldn't lose him, but finally I don't see any car lights following us toward the city.

"What do you mean?" I ask cautiously. I have no idea just how much Beth knows about Calder and Celeste's relationship.

"Look, I know you weren't keen on marrying Jake, but I do think Ben's the better choice for you. He's definitely less *scrappy*."

When Beth lets out a laugh, I realize she's chuckling at her own joke. Jake must be the "Scrappy" she mentioned earlier. Interesting nickname. I don't remember him getting into fights at school, but I didn't go to the football games, so who knows just how rough he was on the field.

Sobering, Beth continues, "As soon as Dad announced your engagement to Ben, Calder looked like someone knocked him in the gut. I saw him slip out the patio door after that. Was there something real going on between you two?"

My stomach plummets. I'm so glad I was too distracted to look his way, because seeing him visibly upset would've destroyed all my composure. I grimace. "I feel so bad. I wish I could call him."

"Why don't you call him now?"

"He'll probably never want to speak to me again anyway, so I deleted his number to keep me from making a fool of myself."

"Really?" Beth rolls her eyes and hands me her phone. "If there was the beginning of something between you two, you at least owe him an apology, Celeste. It's the decent thing to do."

Beth appears to have the compassion gene her sister lacks, making her fairly likable. I take her phone, my brows pulling together. "How did you get his number?"

She grins. "When I teasingly told him I might need a security evaluation, he sincerely offered to give me one. I have to say, Celeste, I didn't mind that delicious hunk of a man leaning in close while I added his info to my contacts one bit. He smells divine."

Annoyed, I pull my phone from my pocket and pretend to add Calder's number to it. Instead, I make sure to block the caller ID before I paste his number into a message to Talia.

GIVE *this to S. Now he can locate C. Don't reply back. This isn't my phone.*

I HIT SEND, then pretend to dial Calder while I'm really deleting the text message from the trash folder. I might not be able to officially apologize to Calder for today's events, but helping Sebastian reconnect with his cousin is my way of putting the one person Calder claims to trust—at least he felt that way four years ago—back in his life.

Holding Beth's gaze, I speak into the silent phone. "Hey, Calder. I hoped you'd answer, but I guess I'll have to leave this on your voicemail. I just wanted to apologize. I had no idea my dad would announce my engagement today of all days. I should've told you about my obligation to the Hemming family. As Carver Enterprises' CEO, I'm obligated to keep my father's wishes of merging our families via marriage. The arrangement was established a long time ago. I hope you can forgive me."

I glance at Beth's bummed expression and sigh as I put my phone back in my pocket. "At least I put it out there."

Disappointment creases Beth's smooth skin and she drums her fingers on the steering wheel. "The point is...you tried." Waving her hand to clear the heaviness in the air, she brightens. "Let's have some fun tonight and forget about regrets and obligations for a bit, agreed?"

"Agreed," I say, nodding.

My stomach tightens as we head into the revitalized area of the Lower East Side. The city has been working hard to spruce it up and turn it into a hip place to eat out. And for the most part it's working. Except at night. Its proximity to the dodgier areas makes it a place you only visit during the day.

Yet here we are, pulling up outside an abandoned warehouse at nine in the evening. Granted, we're not alone. A long line of Audis, BMWs, Jaguars and other high-end cars are waiting behind us to enter the security patrolled parking deck.

We drive under the garage's automatic arm after Beth waves a ticket in front of a sensor, and I say, "Where'd you get that ticket? What is this place, Beth? It's as silent as a tomb."

She parks and cuts the engine. "The ticket tells us where to go. The secret locations change every three months. Just trust me. You needed to get out and cut loose. And I know you, Celeste. This is as far *out* of your comfort zone as you'll ever get."

"That's *not* comforting," I say, following her across the parking lot. Normally I would find my comment amusing. Between Talia and me, I'm usually the more adventurous one, but right now, I'm not technically myself. When we walk in the opposite direction of the elevator that other patrons are waiting for, I tilt my chin toward it. "Um, isn't that the way we're supposed to take?"

Beth giggles and punches a button to a smaller elevator. "Not us. We're extra special VIPs."

"So they're VIPs as well?" I ask Beth as the elevator takes a short trip up. "What kind of place is this?"

"It's called the Elite Underground Club or EUC for short." The second the elevator opens at our destination, the roar of a crowd drowns out the rest of what Beth says.

My jaw drops when she drags me out of the elevator. "You brought me to a fight match?"

I stare at the official-looking fight cage in the center of the room below and the mass of people still pouring in through another entrance. Beth and I are standing on a kind of balcony at the highest point in the room. The only way down to the main floor is via a ramp to our left. The ramp circles the entire massive room all the way down to the main floor, where a couple hundred chairs are set up in a circle around the ring.

Beth lets out a full-bellied laugh. "It was totally worth bringing you here just to see that look on your face. Come on. We need to hurry." Before I can protest, she grabs my hand and pulls me down the ramp.

While we make our way through the crowd of men and women starting to seat themselves, I say over the general murmur of pre-fight talk, "I can't believe how many women are here."

Beth pauses once we reach the center aisle that leads

right up to the stairs outside the cage. "Why? You don't think women can enjoy a good MMA fight?"

I glance around the packed place. "You don't usually see this many women at a boxing match, do you? In the past, women just haven't enjoyed watching violent sports."

"Ha! The times have changed, big sister," Beth says, proceeding down the aisle. "Not only do we enjoy it, we get turned on by it."

I hurry to catch up to her, my eyebrows raised. "Okaaaaay, then. That was TMI, but whatever floats your boat, LL."

Beth's cheeky grin softens. "You haven't called me that in a long time."

The way she's looking at me makes me wonder if I've just blown my own cover, but then Beth throws her arm around my neck and yanks me into a tight hug. Pulling me along, she whispers in my ear, "I kind of miss it."

Relieved I didn't screw up, I smile and elbow her lightly in the ribs. "So do you have extra VIP front row tickets too?"

Beth wrinkles her nose at my teasing before she tugs me into a huge group of girls all calling out to one of the organizers—a beefy bald guy with a hard expression who's wearing a black T-shirt that reads SECURITY in bold white letters.

"Pick me!" A high-pitched voice calls from the gaggle of women.

"No, I'm the one you want!" a perky blonde says.

A tall, busty brunette elbows the short blonde in the

head, and when she screams out, Big Boobs sneers, "See what happens when you pinch people?"

Snickering at them, Beth says to me in a low tone, "We're not sitting. We're joining the greeting party."

I soon discover what the "greeting party" is when the bald guy picks Beth, me, and eight other women, then points to the edge of the stairs leading up to the caged ring and says in a rumbling voice, "Line up on the left side of the aisle, ladies."

Beth giggles mischievously as she pulls me to her left and murmurs, "This is going to be fun."

Standing next to the stairs, I'm at a loss as to what I'm supposed to do. Do we wave and scream for the fighters like cheerleaders? The only reason I was picked is because Beth insisted we were a package deal once the guy chose her. Of course he chose her! She might not be dressed in skimpy skin-tight, mid-drift clothes like the other ladies, but her tall black boots, black mini skirt and fitted red sweater with a deep-vee shows off her assets well. She definitely competes. I feel completely underdressed, but I'm here...may as well get swept up in the fun. I ignore the other girls snorting at my basic outfit and whistle and holler right along with Beth.

The music amps at the same time the lights suddenly dim. A single spotlight focuses on the center aisle and a man's deep voice announces across the speakers. "Are you ready for the championship fight tonight?" The crowd goes nuts, screaming and whistling, while the announcer begins to rattle off fight stats for the first fighter as the spotlight shifts to the top of the aisle where the fighter stands. "Give it up for Stone Cold Jack Hammer!" the announcer finally booms.

Other than the red tape crisscrossed around his hands and fingers, the fighter is wearing a pair of red shorts with a white waistband and no shoes. While he punches one hand into the other and flexes his thick chest and ab muscles, obviously soaking in the moment of undivided attention, I ask Beth, "What's up with that tight mask covering his whole head? It makes me feel like he's going to rob me."

"Ha, yeah, on top of the required use of stage names, the mask's intimidating factor is a side benefit." Beth's chuckle dies down as she leans close to whisper, "Did you notice the guys in suits who walked into that booth?"

I follow her line of sight to a glassed-in sky-box to the right of the elevator where we exited. I can't believe I missed seeing it when we first got off, but then the fight cage pretty much drew my undivided attention. The sky-box glass is tinted so we can't see inside, and several massive guards of different ethnicities stand around the outside of the booth, watching the crowd below with protective scrutiny stamped on their faces. "No, I didn't."

Beth nods and gives a knowing smile. "Those are the true VIPs of the night. The men enter the booth with masks on too, though I hear theirs are more comfortable. They're here to be entertained, but with all that muscle up there protecting them, I'm sure they're men of influence. One thing is for sure...they're staggeringly wealthy. I've heard *those* tickets are over a million each."

I gulp. "A million? How much was our ticket?"

"It was a gift," she titters. "As for the major VIPs up there, my guess is they place massive bets on these fights. This championship bout is the penultimate for the fighters who've worked so hard in the amateur arenas to get chosen for the EUC. Only a few were hand-selected and offered the chance to fight in four bouts total over the course of a year. Three previous elimination bouts lead to this one main event. Tonight's winner will not only be well paid, he'll also get an audience with those men if he chooses."

"I would think the fighters would want all the glory and fame in the arena," I say. "Why wouldn't they want all the fans to know who they are?" Frowning, I continue, "And more importantly...how do you know all this?"

She *tsks* and fluffs her hair. "I have ways to get people to talk. I'm charming like that. And as for the fighters keeping their identities a secret, in the three other EUC fights that lead up to this main event, the fans do get to know the MMA fighters through their stage names." She gestures to the fighter in red shorts who'd stopped to sign autographs on his way toward the ring. "Since only amateur—aka unpaid— MMA fighting is allowed in NY, the fighters' identities are kept secret. They can't get in trouble for being paid if no one knows who they are. The masks protect their identities so they won't have problems with the law, which could hurt them if they wanted to go pro later." She stops talking and laughs at my dumbfounded expression. "Yes, I'm a fan."

"A super fan more like." I snort. "But...headgear aside, wouldn't their stats give them away?"

Beth smirks. "I can tell by their accents that the guys

who fight aren't always native to New York. But since we don't have a name or city to compare their stats to, it would be hard to figure out who the fighter really is."

"Wait...so when they're not fighting for this underground outfit, they fight in amateur bouts here in New York?"

She nods. "At any point an amateur fighter could get picked up to go pro, but this secret organization gives them a chance to make some good money in the interim."

"Illegally," I add with a bit of censure in my tone. "It's amazing how those masks protect not just the fighters but the group sponsoring this event."

Sweeping her hair back over her shoulder, Beth smirks. "Yes, I'm sure that's a very true statement. You know, you should hire one of these guys to be your bodyguard. I mean, look at him? *No* one is going to mess with you if you had someone like that beside you."

He's definitely bulkier than Celeste's guard. The fighter is halfway down the aisle now, so I can finally see what he's carrying. As the spotlight following him shines on us too, I have to shield my eyes to make it out. It's a white carnival-style mask. Just when I start to ask Beth what the mask is for, the bald guy touches the wireless headset on his ear, then immediately narrows his gaze on Celeste's sister.

"Damnit," she mutters when he stalks straight for us.

"Come with me," he says in a clipped tone and grips her arm.

I step out of the line, following him as he leads her away.

"Let go of her!" I try to pry his meaty paw off, but Beth pulls my hand free, laughing. "Don't make a scene, Celeste. My boyfriend's just pissed that I'm standing here. One of these days he's not going to catch me. Go get back in line. I'll be right back."

Her boyfriend? Before I can say anything else, the bald guy hands Beth to another security person and she's escorted into the darkness.

With no ticket for a seat, I step back in line to wait for Beth. Jack Hammer currently has the ladies all stirred up as he makes his way down the line. It's hard not to roll my eyes at the obvious display of cleavage the girls put on when he walks past them.

Once he sees the tall, well-endowed brunette standing next to the short blonde on my right, he stops and grins. Just as he starts to place his white mask on her, he gives the blonde and me an afterthought glance and then suddenly pauses.

Stepping in front of me, he ignores Big Boob's angry wail of frustration and slips the mask on my face. Tracing my cheek with his thumb, he tilts my chin up and says, "Meet me after."

Before I can tell him that I *won't* be meeting him later, he starts up the stairs. As soon as he steps into the fight cage, the crowd explodes with excitement.

While everyone's cheering as he raises his arms and circles the ring, getting the audience hyped-up, someone yanks hard on my hair. "Ow!" With unshed tears stinging my eyes, I glare over my shoulder at Busty Girl.

"What are you looking at, midget?" she snaps, her chest puffed out in bully mode.

I narrow my gaze. "Don't touch me again, or you'll go home with deflated boobs."

Sneering, she folds her arms over her fake breasts, but the announcer coming back on the speaker drowns out her words. "And tonight's next fighter is Steel, aka Fists of Steel. This man has moved up fast in the amateur MMA ranks, his bout stats earning him a coveted spot in Elite Underground Club's tournament bracket when Ramp, aka Rampage, had to drop out earlier this year."

While the announcer continues on about the contending fighter standing up at the top of the aisle in black shorts and a black mask, the bald security guy retrieves a stack of round cards the size of a stop sign from one of the men manning the judges' area right in front of the cage. Handing the angry brunette a card marked with the number one, he says, "Take the first round, ring girl, and stop complaining or you'll be banned from EUC for good." Ignoring her unappreciative "ugh", he gives four other girls the rest of the signs numbered two through five.

Sighing her frustration that she didn't get picked to be a ring girl either, the blonde next to me whispers in my ear, "Better watch your back. Amanda has had her eye on Jack Hammer all season. The fact he not only picked you over her, but invited you to be with him later...she'll be after you for stealing him from her."

I grip her arm. "Wait...be with him. As in have sex with him?"

Her blue eyes flutter, appearing extra large on her petite face. "Every once in a while the fighter will ask the girl to stay. That's code for...he wants you. The rules are super clear though...neither of you can take your masks off. Oh, I'm Tilly by the way." I start to say my name, but she quickly turns away as the other fighter comes within yelling distance. "Steel, pick me, baby!"

Who would have sex with someone whose face they'll never see? This can't be what Beth intended. She might not be my real little sister, but that's nuts. I need to talk to her. I try to step out of the line, but a group of girls have crowded behind me in an effort to get a closer look at Steel. I'm forced to stay put while the fighter turns to shake someone's hand and sign several fans' tickets. The ink covering his entire back draws my attention, and, just like the girls tittering all around me, I can't help but stare.

A massive bird's wing spans between his shoulder blades and around his left shoulder. The black ink feathers unfurl down the left half of his body from the middle of his broad back, around his sinuously muscled arm and along his ribcage. Taking up the entire right side of his back is an amazingly realistic half skull that starts just below the few feathers touching his right shoulder. Deep eye-sockets lead to hollowed-out cheekbones just above a toothy mouth. The impressive ink follows the slabs of muscle along Steel's lower back before disappearing into his black shorts. The realization that the skull's chin must curve around the top part of muscular butt cheeks makes my stomach clench in full appreciation. That's a hell of a tattoo.

I whisper to Tilly, "Someone must know who he is. His tattoos are a work of art and highly memorable."

She shakes her head in fast jerks. "No one knows. Believe me, I've asked. He must've gotten tattooed right after he signed up for this years' EUC tournament and has only fought in those bouts so far. Here he comes!"

The Fists of Steel contender only has a couple inches on Jack Hammer, but his bearing is far more menacing. Unlike Hammer, who obviously likes the showmanship of the fight, this guy holds himself with the presence of a street fighter. Like he's seen his fair share of no-holds-barred, bare-knuckle fighting.

Pulse thrumming, I fold my fingers around the edge of Jack Hammer's mask, intending to give it to Tilly. But something about this Steel guy's intimidating look as he walks down the line of girls makes me decide to leave the flimsy layer of protection on until he passes by and enters the cage.

My heart rate jolts to mock speed when Steel stops in front of me. *Why is he staring at me like a lion about to pounce?* It doesn't help that the fans are calling out, "He's looking at your girl, Hammer!"

Hammer walks up to the cage's closed door and scowls at Steel, a blatant threat in his eyes. *Don't fucking look at her.*

Steel grunts and whisks the white mask off me, tossing it behind him in an open challenge.

The crowd goes wild and Tilly grabs my arm, squealing in my ear. "Oh my God, Hammer's arguing with the EUC's official to let him out!"

I hear Tilly, but I can't look away from the fighter in front of me, nor do I give a flip that Big Boobs Amanda is scrambling to pick up the white mask he dropped. As soon as he took my mask off, Steel's mouth shifted from a smartass smirk to a thin, hard line. *Why does he look pissed? Maybe he thought I was better looking under the mask.* I push my shoulders back and tilt my chin up.

Sliding his black carnival mask into place on my face, Steel cups the back of my head and says in a low, harsh rumble, "You're mine."

This might be pure entertainment for everyone else—his action ramping the fans while also giving a big "fuck you" to Hammer—but not for me. I rip the mask off and toss it behind me to the gaggle of girls. While the crowd goes even nuttier over my apparent rejection, and the girls squeal and fight over the black mask like a bride's bouquet, I hold his suddenly narrowed gaze. "No one owns me. Not him. Not you."

He takes a deep breath, his chest widening as he pulls something from his short's pocket. Dropping the beaded steel chain around my neck, he rumbles in a coarse tone, "Don't fucking take this off."

Anger erupts and I quickly grab the tape-covered metal dangling from the chain. Before I can take it off, Steel pulls my hand free of the necklace and slides his other hand under my hair, touching the back of my neck. The black tape on his hand rubs mine as he presses my fingers to the side of his neck and bites out in a gruff tone just for my ears, "Keep it on. I'm *not* asking."

With all the shouting going on around us, my self-preservation meter is screaming at me to pull away. But something in the tightness of his hold on my hand draws my attention to his neck. I look up to see two familiar sharp points just above my fingers that he's pressing against his pulse and my stomach drops.

Calder?

My gaze jerks to his, seeking confirmation to my unspoken recognition. When our eyes meet, I finally reconcile what my mind was too distracted to see a few seconds ago. Calder's green eyes boring into me, full of anger, judgment, and guarded heat.

Pressing his lips together, he releases me without another word and walks up the stairs and into the cage.

CHAPTER SEVENTEEN

CALDER

*W*hat the hell is she doing here? My stomach tenses with worry as I glance back. She's standing there gripping my dog tags, a shocked expression on her face. Something is definitely going on with her, and my life is beyond screwed up, yet I thought for sure she was sincere when we were in the garden together today.

Hearing her say that our connection was as strong as ever was enough to temporarily stave off my questions, but watching her get engaged fifteen minutes later was more shit than I could deal with. Not when this bout was hanging over my head. Everything I've worked toward comes down to this fight. I needed space to get my head right, not to mention...I didn't want her anywhere near this part of my life.

I only intended to rile Hammer by taking whichever ring girl he'd picked. But when I pulled his damn mask off, she's the last person I expected to see. This is so royally fucked up, but now that she's in my domain, everyone has to know that she's mine. No one better fucking touch her.

The second I enter the cage and the door closes, I shut-down the worry slamming through my head and turn to face Hammer.

"You're dead!" he yells over the screaming crowd. Fury is evident in his tight fists and pinched mouth as he watches the tall brunette wearing his white mask while she saunters the full circle around the outside of the cage, the round number one sign high above her head.

That's exactly how I want him. Pissed as hell. I've worked too damn hard to fuck this up now. He might want the glory, but he's about to find out I'm far hungrier for this win.

I studied his other fights; Hammer hits hardest when he's angry. Works for me. I've been itching for someone to challenge me enough to make all this bullshit worth the past six months. Her rejection at the party earlier threw me off, but now that she's here, I'm so damned amped up at the idea of her being there once this event is over.

Hope is a concept I'd given up on. I know it's illogical to think she's here for me. She definitely didn't recognize me in this mask, but a part of me can't help but believe her being here wasn't just a coincidence. The powerful combination of protectiveness and hope are a jolt of pure adrenaline to my system. Pounding this prick into the mat will be the perfect release for me. I jam my mouth guard in and pull on my gloves.

When the ref signals the fight to begin, I lift my hands, then curl my fingers toward me and give Hammer a sharp look that says, "Bring it, asshole."

CHAPTER EIGHTEEN

CASS

I can't help but wince when Hammer goes after Steel like a rampaging bull, fists flying. Calder pounds him back with several swift punches and knee jabs to the ribs. I'm still trying to process the fact that the guy I thought for sure was a street fighter is Calder.

Tilly is clapping loudly and yelling for Steel to kick Hammer's ass. No doubt who she's cheering for. When she taps me on the shoulder and says, "Let's see it," I frown in confusion.

"See what?"

She tosses her long hair over her shoulder and points to Calder's dog tags still clenched in my hand. "Peel back the tape he's wrapped around those tags. Let's find out his real name."

Shit, I didn't even think about the fact that I'm wearing his real identity around my neck.

"Um, I think Steel might want to go a few rounds in the cage with me if I even thought about touching the tape. Sorry, Tilly."

She sighs her understanding, then returns her attention to the fight, screaming, "Give the Hammer a spinning back-fist!"

She sure is bloodthirsty for such a tiny thing. Of course I can't help but wonder why Calder is here in the first place. He doesn't need the money. As I watch Hammer land a punch to Calder's jaw and his head snaps sideways, anger lashes through me. I jump in with Tilly and yell for him to take Hammer down while he's got Hammer in what Tilly is calling a guillotine choke. *Why the hell is Calder putting his life at risk?* It can't possibly be for glory. He didn't even seem to care about that.

The men break apart and circle the mat, fists up in guarded positions while they look for ways to pound the shit out of each other.

Suddenly Hammer comes at Steel with a rapid round of punches. Calder steps back and shakes his head, and then jumps in the air with a spin kick. He takes Hammer down to the mat in a move that stuns the hell out of me.

The battle of wills continues on the mat as Hammer tries to break free. But the round goes to Steel as the bell rings.

"Did you see that? I don't even know what that was!" Tilly asks the girl next to her for her take.

"I think it was a double spin kick. Holy shit that was one of the best takedowns I've ever seen."

The crowd rushes to their feet, some roaring for Steel, others for Hammer. Everyone is excited. All too soon, round two starts up and my stomach coils into knots all over again.

When the ref calls the round to start, Hammer charges at Calder once again. That must be his signature move, trying to throw his opponent off his game. But Calder just bats him away like an annoying fly.

My ears ring with the screams from the girls all around me. I feel the slightest bit dizzy. I don't want to watch Calder get punched in the head all for sport. Pulling my phone out I quickly text Beth.

Where the heck are you?

I'm standing beside my boyfriend. Speaking of...he wants me to go to an after party with him. You game?

Who knows how long the after party will last. I need to be ready to leave when Celeste calls. I shoot a message back.

I'll pass. Don't worry. I'll just grab a cab.

Are you sure? You can take my car and Brent can bring me home.

I remember seeing a few people getting dropped off by cabs as we pulled into the garage.

Yep, I'm good.

Okay, if you're sure. Hope you're having fun down there. Did you enjoy being fought over by both fighters? That has never happened before!

I grimace. *Um, that's not something I want to experience again.*

LOL! Only you would find being fought over by two

hunky men an experience you don't want to repeat. Sheesh, girl! See you at home.

I start to type her a response and my phone's battery dies. *You've got to be kidding me.* I try to turn it off, then back on, but it's officially dead. I can't believe I didn't think to charge the phone, but then again, I didn't expect to have it this long. Just as I look up, the bout ends, and the round goes to Hammer, who's apparently acting more than a bit crazed.

After the ring girl does her walk around the catwalk around the outside of the cage, round three begins.

Only this time, the tone of the fight changes. In the last round, Hammer was relentless, but in this one, he doesn't seem to be fighting with the same vigor. Is he exhausted? He doesn't appear to be out of breath or anything. But at this rate, Calder is clearly going to win this round by sheer strikes and general fight control. I exhale a relieved breath. Calder just has to win the bout after this one and the fight is over.

Calder looks like he could go another ten rounds without breaking a sweat, but I don't like watching someone trying to beat the snot out of him either. Hammer's hits have to hurt like hell.

Suddenly Calder hooks his leg on Hammer's and swipes his feet out from under him. They both go down, and while they're grappling on the mat, he says something that sets Hammer off. With a roaring growl, Hammer literally tosses Calder across the mat.

When Calder turns and faces Hammer and I see him

smile around his mouth guard, I realize Calder antagonized his opponent on purpose.

Ugh, he had *this round. Does the man have a death wish?*

Hammer swings a hard right and punches Calder so hard he slams into the cage. I gasp and squeeze the dog tags, worry for Calder ripping through me. Calder ducks Hammer's next swing and twists, landing a spinning back fist into Hammer's jaw that sends the guy stumbling back.

Shaking off the grogginess, Hammer roars. Just as he starts across the mat for Calder, the lights flash and the announcer comes over the speaker. "We've just learned the police are on their way. No need to rush. There's enough time to get to your cars. The championship EUC will be rescheduled soon. Look for your tickets to arrive."

Of course no one listens to the announcer. Pandemonium breaks out. The security guys try to maintain order, but people flood into the main aisle in an effort to get to the exit as fast as possible. Tilly grabs my hand and tries to tug me along with her, but someone pulls my arm free of her hold. I get a glimpse of vengeful eyes in a white mask as Amanda shoves me against the stair rail leading up to the cage. While pain racks my ribs and air whooshes out of my lungs, she laughs and turns away into the moving mass. I try to recover and go after her, but too many people crowd in at once, jamming me against the railing.

Panic takes over when it gets harder to take a breath. I contemplate trying to squeeze through the narrow stair railing and take a chance getting stuck, when someone yells above me, "Give me your hands."

I glance up to see Calder looking at me over the rail. "Trust me to keep you safe," he says gruffly and holds his hands out.

As soon as I lift my hands up, he plucks me out of the crowd like I weigh nothing. He moves so fast, I'm hauled over the railing and set on the stairs before I can get my bearings.

"This way," he rumbles and takes my hand, tugging me behind him.

We move past the cage's opening, and I have to hurry to keep up with Calder's long strides as we cross the mat. Pushing open another door on the opposite side of the cage, Calder quickly jumps down from the catwalk area, landing five-feet below with the grace of a bounding tiger. Turning quickly, he says, "Sit and I'll lift you down."

I've barely touched my butt to the floor's edge when he grips my waist. Once he lowers me to the floor in front of him, he cups my face. "I'm sorry you got slammed into the railing. The lock on the main entrance kept me from getting to you faster. Are you okay to walk?"

I'm still shaking, but I'm glad we're away from the mass of people on the other side of the cage. I nod and ignore the dull throb radiating from my ribcage. "I'll be fine, but..." I pause and glance toward the exit. "The last thing I want to do is head back into that mad crush."

Calder flashes a smile. "You won't have to. Come on."

He pulls me over to another door and pushes it open. As I follow him down a dark hallway, lit only by a stairwell sign at the end of the hall, I wonder if the other fighter and referee fled into the crowd or if they took this same path. By Calder's movements, he seems intent on being as quiet as possible, so I don't ask.

Opening a door in the hallway, he grabs a duffle bag sitting just inside and rips open the zipper. Once he tugs off his mask and wipes his face with a towel, he stows his mask, then slides a pair of scissors under the black tape and gauze on his hand, quickly cutting it away. After he's taken care of the other hand, he pulls on a white T-shirt and a pair of running shoes.

It's so nice to see his whole face, I can't help but smile despite the fact the police could raid the place at any moment. Without a word, I follow him down a stairwell and out the backside of the building.

After ten minutes of brisk walking between some adjacent abandoned buildings, Calder stops beside a black truck and opens the passenger door for me.

"Why didn't you park in the deck like everyone else?" I ask once we pull away from the curb.

He glances my way and smirks. "I'm sure the car line out of the deck is still going right now, but mostly it's to keep my anonymity."

"Ah, Beth mentioned the reason for the masks. *Beth*...crap."

Worried for Beth, I pull my phone out of my pocket, then remember it's dead. "You um, don't happen to have a charger in your car, do you?"

Glancing at my phone, he shakes his head. "Not with me. My phone's at my place. You can plug your phone in when you get there. As for Beth, I'm sure she's fine. I guarantee the place will be completely emptied out before the police arrive."

The last is said with such sarcasm, I glance up from trying once more to turn my phone on. "How can you be so sure?"

He faces toward the road and tightens his hold on the steering wheel. "Because too much money runs through this EUC group to let something as pesky as a police raid get in the way of their bottom line."

"Wait...are you saying they have the police in their back pocket?"

"Amongst others," he says in a dry tone.

"Why would you be involved with a group like that, Calder? You're better than that."

He cuts a cold gaze my way. "What makes you think I'm better? My last name? It sure as fuck wasn't good enough for you earlier today."

I open my mouth to deny his assumption, but then shut it. I deserve that. Well, Celeste does anyway. But the truth is...how well do I know him? Not at all, really. But I thought I had a sense of the kind of person he was four years ago. He's obviously changed a lot since then. More than anyone in his family knows, apparently.

"I'm sorry, Calder. On too many fronts to count," I say sincerely, glancing out the window at the streetlights zooming past. "Thank you for saving me tonight. You didn't have to. *That's* what makes you better."

"I might not be a Blake 'golden boy' any longer, but

helping you was my only option," he says quietly as he pulls up outside an apartment building just on the edge of the revitalized Lower East End.

Why does he think his family no longer sees him in good light? According to Talia, he's the one who has kept his distance. Not the other way around.

Calder's apartment is surprisingly neat when we walk in. It's also no more than four hundred square feet, but he somehow makes the kitchen/living/bedroom combo work by using his coffee table as a dining table and pushing his bed against the big glass window to give him as much "living space" as possible. An extra long, old leather couch sections off his sleeping area from the living space very well.

"You've made the most of this space," I say in a quiet voice, appreciating the old vinyl albums and record player taking up bookshelf slots below two rows of leather bound books. He's a vintage guy. *I freaking love that!*

Calder walks over to the bookshelves and pulls open a drawer underneath the record player. Retrieving a cord, he attaches something onto the end of it, then holds it out. "I think this adapter should work for your phone."

"Thanks." I take the cord and plug it into the outlet shared by the record player. As I slide the other end of the cord into my phone and the screen lights up with the charging icon, I'm acutely aware of Calder's stare following every move I make and hyper-sensitive to the fact we're both not talking about my surprise engagement.

I note the lock screen, but hold out hope it's just part of the start up sequence. Setting my phone on the shelf, I smile at the record player, then glance at the stack of albums. I almost ask if he minds if I look through them, but what if Celeste hates this kind of music or he's already shown her his collection?

So instead I lean back against the wall and sigh. "I guess my phone was deader than I realized. The reboot will take a few minutes."

Calder rests his hand on the wall next to me at the same time he lifts his dog tags from my chest.

"Oh, sorry." When I move to take it off, Calder captures the chain in his hand so I can't touch it.

"It looks good on you," he says in a low tone. Stepping closer, he wraps the chain around his fist, tightening it. Stroking his thumb along my collarbone, he continues, his voice thick with tension. "You have no idea how seeing my dog tags around your neck jacks me up." He twists his hand until it's taut and I'm forced even closer. "Today should never have happened...ever!"

His whole body is tense with simmering anger, but as much as Celeste deserves it, I don't. I blink back the emotion rising to the surface, then lift my gaze to his. "Then why didn't you fight for me, Calder?"

He smirks and slides his thumb along my quivering bottom lip. "I did. Hammer wasn't going to give you up."

I shake my head. "I'm not talking about the fight."

Capturing my chin in a firm hold, his amused expression disappears. "Why would you agree to marry Ben right after you told me how you felt about us in the garden?" He slides his fingers down the side of my throat, then presses them against my pulse. "Your pulse is racing, angel. Everything else out of your mouth might be a lie, but your reaction when I touch you isn't. You still want me."

Everything else? What is he talking about? I'm desperate to spill my guts about who I really am. Celeste doesn't deserve my loyalty. I could care less about mending her relationship with Calder, but I made this stupid deal, not just for my father's sake, but for my sister's. I promised and I don't go back on my word. Ever.

I have to see it through no matter how much I hate that Calder is getting the brunt of Celeste's selfishness. I'm sure if he ever learns about me when this is all over, he'll never forgive me, but I can at least apologize to him the way Celeste should have already. She owes him that much.

"My marriage to Ben is purely a business arrangement. It's something the Carvers and the Hemming family agreed on a long time ago. As CEO of Carver Enterprises, I'm obligated to follow through. I had no idea my father would decide to make the announcement tonight. I'm sorry you had to find out like that. The last thing I wanted to do was hurt you."

He tilts my chin up, his gaze narrowed. "I meant what I said earlier. You're mine. I'm no longer a better man, angel. I have every intention of fucking you into sheer exhaustion until you come to your senses and break off this goddamn sham of an engagement."

The determined ruthlessness in his gaze knots my stomach with both desire and apprehension. As much as I want to let him fulfill every erotic promise he just made—

God, I so want him to—I refuse to have sex with him as Celeste. What happened between us at the party four years ago was the last thing I expected, but it became a memory I've never been able to let go.

Calder is an even more intriguing and multifaceted man than I ever imagined. *He* means something to me, but he doesn't even freaking know the real me exists. Fury rips through me at my untenable situation. I need to get the hell out of here. If Calder starts to follow through on his plans, I'm too emotionally connected and I'll just complicate things even further than I already have.

I need to take back the reins of this conversation and steer it to more even ground.

I glance toward the duffle bag he dropped near the door. "For someone who demands full disclosure, it appears you had your own secrets. I remember you saying once that there would be no more costumes, no masks, and no fake names between us, *Steel*."

He puts his other hand on the wall and lowers his handsome face close to mine. His light brown hair is a mess, and the sight of his overnight beard makes my stomach clench in excitement despite my vow to remain unaffected. "I was referring to us, and you damn well know it."

"You're the last person I expected to see. Beth brought me. Does she know you're Steel?"

"No," he murmurs as he inhales in a slow, tantalizing circle around my mouth. "You smell so fucking good."

His comment clenches my insides, reminding me of our brief time together. I hate that he can't tell that I smell different. It's not like he's an animal with keen olfactory senses, but still it would be nice if he could somehow know that I'm me and not *her*. I sigh inwardly as I take in his masculine scent of soap and sweat. My heart ramps when his lips stop just in front of mine. I know it's wrong, but I can't stop myself from wanting him to kiss me.

"In the interest of full disclosure," he begins in a low, husky rasp, his mouth brushing torturously close to mine.

"Yes?" I breathe out, completely under his seductive spell.

He suddenly straightens and lifts his muscular arms behind him, tugging his T-shirt off in one swift movement. I'm so mesmerized by the wing tattoo curving around the left half of his body that I don't protest as he drags me over to the bathroom door.

When he walks into the bathroom, rips back the curtain and turns on the shower, I shake my head. "I'm not taking a shower with you."

"I didn't ask you to," he says, kicking off his shoes.

I furrow my brow, confused. "Then why—" I start to ask, but instantly turn away when he yanks down his shorts, stripping completely naked. "Wh—what are you doing?"

He touches my jaw and forces me to face the bathroom once more. "I'm giving you what you asked for. But you'll have to look to understand."

I meet his steady gaze and wish the bathroom light wasn't so bright. He has to see how red my cheeks are. I'm not usually embarrassed by the sight of a naked man. I've seen my fair share, but for some reason Calder seems to be able to ferret out the weakest sides of me, those insecure parts that want to remain hidden away. Even though I'm fully clothed, I feel like I'm the one exposed right now.

The sound of the water turning on draws my gaze. Once I get a full view of his back as he leans in to check the water's temperature, I can't look away. His body is truly a breathtaking work of art; powerful, sinuous back muscles add realistic dimension to the skull. The dark-themed tattoo gives him a dangerously mysterious and edgy vibe, and I was right—the skull ends right at the top of his ass, drawing my gaze to the two perfectly formed globes of muscle. God I wish I had my camera. I'd put it on black and white mode and drink him in through the lens. But these pictures would only be for Raven's personal collection.

"Have you got your fill yet?"

The arrogant amusement in his voice draws my attention. As heat rides my cheeks once more, I lean against the doorjamb and gesture to the shower, letting my sarcasm fly. "Other than a blatant show of exhibitionism, I fail to see how me watching you take a shower answers anything."

"Other than a blatant act of voyeurism on *your* part, full disclosure is coming, angel." Smirking, he picks up a bottle of body soap then starts to drizzle it over his shoulders and down his back. The second the water hits the strong herbal smelling soap on his inked skin, a streak of flesh shows through.

It's not real? I instantly straighten and blink to make sure I'm not seeing things. *Holy shit!* I want to ask tons of questions, but I can't bring myself to break the spell as

Calder washes away the massive tattoo from his back. While a part of me is glad he won't be carrying around such darkness inked on his skin for the rest of his life, another slightly selfish part of me wishes he would've kept at least some of the wing across his upper back. *What does it mean to him?*

As the black ink sloughs off his skin and swirls into the drain, I can't help but fancifully hope it's his symbolic way of shedding the loner persona that has kept him from his family. I truly wish that for him.

Calder turns and faces me as he continues to wash away the massive tattoo on his muscular left shoulder and hard pectoral. My gaze greedily follows his fingers massaging the suds down his arm and along his waist and flexing ab muscles.

My skin prickles with heat and my belly clenches as I follow his hand brushing over his skin. I want to be the one washing the dirty water away. I would revel in touching him so freely and intimately. I force myself to breathe slowly to keep from panting, but the pull he has over me is unlike anything I've ever felt. The desperate need to step forward and touch him is so strong, I grab the doorjamb and take several deep breaths to keep me in place.

As my libido settles, I realize that some of the ink on his shoulder and arm isn't disappearing. Instead, amid the suds and streaming water, I see ink starting to darken against newly revealed skin, forming some kind of distinct pattern. While I hold my breath in anticipation, a memory of panning for gold with my family suddenly comes to me. When I was ten, Dad took us to Colorado. Sophie and I stood in that cool water sifting through dirt for what felt like hours, but when a few glimmers of gold appeared against the screen in my hand, I'd never been more excited.

That same sense of discovering something special flows through me now as a unique Celtic tribal design appears on Calder, curving around his left shoulder and halfway down his forearm. The pattern continues along his rib cage where the word "Solus" stands against his skin in perfect clarity.

God, he's a beautiful man. He might not think he's the family's Golden Boy any longer, but he's mine. And *this* tattoo means something to him, every part of it.

With another round of soap, Calder runs his hand over his skin and along his ribs. When his movements slow and his hand travels past his hip to fist his full erection, in that split second I can't look away. My heart rate hikes as he slides his hand up and down his cock with measured, deliberate purpose. I'm sure if I look up and meet his heated gaze, he'll tell me to join him, but I can't force my eyes upward. I want him too much. Swallowing hard, I step out of the bathroom.

As the shower shuts off, I lean against the wall and close my eyes. When I feel the heat of Calder's presence in front of me a few seconds later, I finally open my eyes. "Though it's nice to know you won't have a skull on your back indefinitely, what was the point of that," I say in a tight voice.

Calder's sporting a pair of soft gray jersey pants. They sit low on his hips, drawing attention to his rock-hard abs and the slabs of muscle that disappear beneath the waistband. When my attention zeroes in on the bruising along his ribcage and the welt curving over the top of his left hipbone, my heart constricts. I shift my gaze to his face to keep from thinking about him getting really hurt. Water still drips from his tousled hair, streaking down the sides of his face and into his overnight beard.

Sliding his fingers under my hair, he rests his hand on the back of my neck. "This is full disclosure time, angel."

I hate that he calls Celeste *angel*. Hearing him say it to her stirs swift fury in my chest despite the heat of his fingers sliding into my hair. I want to ask him about his real tattoo, but *Celeste* would already know of its existence, so I hold back. I need to keep our conversation away from intimate issues.

I lift my gaze, intending to ask why he kept his fighting a secret, but he steps close and presses his mouth to mine in a heart-stopping kiss.

When you want something bad enough, not even a Mac truck carrying a full load of well-intended principles can pull you away. I've wanted to feel his mouth on mine again after all this time that, for a moment, my lips part and I let him in.

The sensation of his tongue twining with mine is so deliciously perfect and enticingly seductive, I whimper against his mouth. When his knuckles brush against my breast as he begins to unbutton the top button on my shirt, my adrenaline spikes. I ache to feel his hot skin and muscular chest pressed against mine. He makes fast work of the buttons and my shirt quickly falls open. Powerful hands grip my upper back and I'm lifted completely off the ground as his hot mouth connects with the curve of my breast above my bra.

Calder sets me against the wall and glides his tongue around the chain on my neck and down my cleavage before slowly tasting me all the way up my neck. Once he reaches my ear, he boldly bites the soft lobe, then rumbles against my jaw, "I hope you're all caught up on your sleep, because I'm going to devour every fucking inch of your sweet body. Wrap those gorgeous legs around me and hold on."

As he steps into me and trails his tongue back down my chest, I fold my legs around his hips and slide my fingers into his hair. He nips at the fleshy curve of my breast, then does the same to the other before sliding his tongue past my bra and flicking it against my nipple. I squeeze my thighs around his waist as his erection presses against me, the thin material of his pants doing little to keep his hard cock from nudging past my skimpy underwear. My channel floods with want and my fingers twist in the wet locks, pulling him even closer.

Calder groans his approval just before he sucks my nipple into his mouth. Clamping down on me hard, he takes me deep into his mouth with no hesitation. I gasp in sheer bliss and lock my ankles around his muscular backside, allowing myself to just feel.

When he begins to slide my bra strap and shirt down my shoulder, my conscience slams back to reality and my heart suddenly feels like it's breaking apart. Half is being tugged toward him, while the other half resents that he's pressing his magnificent body against Celeste so intimately.

I never wanted to know this much about *their* sex life. I push on his shoulders. "We have to stop, Calder. This can't happen."

Calder lifts his head, his brow furrowed. Setting me down, he frowns past his elevated breathing. "Why not?"

I can't look him in the eye while I pull my bra strap and shirt back into place, but he hooks his thumb on my jaw and forces me to face him. "I've wanted you for four years. I think I've waited long enough."

I'm focused on his jawline, my heart racing crazily, but his comment instantly pulls my gaze to his. "What? But we've already..."

He slowly trails his knuckles along my cheekbone. "Already what?"

"You know," I say, gesturing awkwardly between us. His eyebrow hikes, as if he's waiting for me to continue. "Been intimate," I breathe out uncomfortably.

He shakes his head as he begins to unravel the tape from his dog tags around my neck. Once both tags are tape free, he tosses the balled up black tape over his shoulder and says, "No, we haven't and right now it's one of my biggest regrets."

They never had sex? I'm going to kill Celeste for letting me believe more had gone on between them. More importantly, I don't want him to be with *her* now, but ugh...I can't be with him as me. I want to scream my frustration. This *right here* is definitely Celeste's vengeance on me.

I quickly tug my shirt closed over my chest. "We can't, Calder."

He scowls, clearly annoyed. "Why are you running from us?"

I press my lips together, then exhale, looking away. "I just...can't."

"I've *never* stopped wanting you, Raven," he says in a fierce tone, his thumb sliding behind my ear.

The fact he used the name I gave him at the party for the first time snags my attention. When my gaze jerks back to his, Calder's harsh expression settles as he cups my jaw. "I know you're not Celeste."

He knows? Even though my heart soars, a part of me panics. *What if Celeste finds out? I can't let her back out of our deal.* I need to buy myself time to think through what this means. "I—I don't understand."

His green gaze drills into me. "You could play her, but Celeste could never play you. I knew when I went to the Carver estate to apologize for not contacting you, that she wasn't the woman I was with at that party." His hold tightens slightly on my jaw. "Who is marrying Ben?"

I swallow the lump of anxiety trying to crowd my throat. "Celeste is."

He visibly relaxes and his assessing gaze slowly slides over my face, taking in every facet. "I'll admit the resemblance is scary close, but her eyes don't sparkle like yours do. The moment you turned around at the party today, I instantly recognized you. What is your real name? Are you Celeste's secret twin that no one knows about, and why are you going around pretending to be her?"

I shake my head. "We're not related. I've only pretended to be Celeste twice. The night I met you and today."

"Why?"

I shrug. "The first time was a bit of payback for something from the past."

"And today," he asks, eyebrows raised.

"I can't say."

His gaze narrows. "You can't or you won't?"

I can't chance Celeste not following through for my father, so I take the offensive against his determined line of questioning. "If you knew Celeste wasn't the person you were with at the party four years ago, then why did you date her?"

When he doesn't immediately answer, I realize that we both have things we don't want to talk about. I should leave while my emotions are only slightly trampled. Shrugging out of his hold, I tug my shirt fully closed. "I—I need to go." I quickly button it back up and head in the direction of my cell phone.

Calder grabs my hand before I take three steps and turns me around. "Celeste and I never dated. I had my reasons for sticking around when I realized she wasn't you, but our friendship was just that."

I don't like that he doesn't elaborate on what those reasons were. Plus, if he really wanted to find me, he could've contacted Sebastian at any time to find out my real identity through Talia, but he didn't. Maybe he started to have feelings for Celeste and doesn't want to admit it. I pull my hand free. "If Celeste didn't mean anything to you, then why did you look so upset when she got engaged? Why did you leave without saying anything?"

"I left because it was *you* up there agreeing to marry someone else, not her." Touching my cheek, his tone softens. "You're the one I want; a girl I only know as Raven."

My heart melts and I cup my hand over his. "Will you be okay with just knowing that about me for today?" When he starts to shake his head, I say, "I gave my word, Calder. And if there's one thing you *need* to know about me, it's that I wouldn't exist without it."

Setting his jaw, he pulls me against him and I can't help the small gasp that escapes at the feel of his hard body pressed along mine once more. "Are you in any danger?" When I shake my head, he continues, "Then I can wait...if you tell me one truth about you that no one else knows."

Loving his protective nature, I rise up on my tiptoes and cup the back of his neck to whisper in his ear, "You were my first."

Before I can settle back on my feet, Calder grips my waist, his gaze laser focused and tone crisp. "There's no way you were a virgin to oral sex. Not the way you moved. You knew exactly what you wanted."

With my feet barely touching the ground, I grip his shoulders to stay balanced. "I wasn't new to sex, oral or otherwise. I'm saying you gave me my first real orgasm."

His brow furrows for a second, then disbelief filters through his features before smug arrogance settles. "I would say it's a shame that you went that long without one, but damn if I'll lie. I fucking love that I'm the one who gave you your first."

Definitely the first one I truly wanted.

"Yeah well, I had a few issues in the past." Touching his chest, I smile to keep any dark thoughts of Jake from ruining the moment between us. "And I'd really like to know that it wasn't a fluke. Do you still have that one-hundred-percent satisfaction rating?"

CHAPTER NINETEEN

CASS

"*A* fluke?" An insulted look registers for a split second before my comment sinks in. "Wait...you haven't had one since then?"

His half laugh sets my cheeks on fire. *Great, he's laughing at me and probably thinks I'm a freak too.* A pinging sound saves me from having to answer. Walking over to my phone, I flippantly call over my shoulder, "I'm so glad that amuses you. Why don't you share that 'full disclosure' you were going on about." I pick up my phone and the lock screen mocks me. I try a couple of different combinations, then sigh at my failure to access it.

Calder's silence is deafening, so I ramble while fiddling with the phone's volume button to cover how absolutely inadequate I feel. "I understand the fake tattoo was to hide your real one, but why are you doing underground fighting in the first place? With your skills, I don't understand why you aren't working with your cousin's security firm." The bruising I noticed on his ribs spurs me on. "At least a role like that wouldn't inflict constant damage to your body."

I jump when Calder's warm body presses against my back. "I wasn't laughing at you, Raven. I was reveling in my good fortune."

"What good fortune?" I snort, feeling like he's humoring me.

"The fact that I'll get to be your first in so many more ways," he says right before he quickly lowers something black in front of me, then hooks a choker-style necklace around my neck. As my fingers instantly move to touch the piece of metalwork in the center of the half-inch wide leather around my neck, he continues, "I've had this for a while. I couldn't wait to put it on you."

He turns me to the side so I face the mirror lining the back wall of the bookcase. As my trembling fingers slide over the flying raven slider on the soft leather, his gaze snags mine in the mirror. "The raven needed just the right choker. All I had to do was think of us and it came to me."

Pressing a kiss to my neck, he slides his lips down my throat, murmuring, "I'm looking forward to claiming owner-ship over every single orgasm, angel."

I can't stop staring at his gift. The emotion that clogs my throat makes it hard to breathe. The raven is majestic in flight and the leather is so soft, but also strong. It's a badass necklace and one I definitely would've chosen on my own if I'd run across such a unique piece, because it would remind me of Calder and our time together that night. But what makes tears blur my vision is the fact that leather is something Celeste would never have worn. "It's...perfect," I say, sniffing back my tears.

Calder turns me around, his hands clasping my shoulders. "We connected that night and I had planned to find you, but I didn't want you anywhere near this fighting stuff. Seeing you there tonight freaked me the fuck out. This Elite group is dangerous. I want you to promise me you'll never go back to another fight."

"If they're so dangerous, what are you doing there? You don't need the money; you're a Blake for Pete's sake." I ignore the muscle jumping along his jaw. "And if it's about earning your own way, call Sebastian."

His fingers flex against my shoulders. "It's complicated."

"Then un-complicate it for me." I touch the bruises on his ribs and hate when he tries not to flinch. "Fighting for a group you know is dangerous is no way to live, Calder."

"And pretending to be someone you're not *is*?" he shoots back, folding his muscular arms against his chest.

I know he's angry that I won't tell him my name, but I'm bound by my word. Reaching up, I flatten my palm against his pectoral. He tenses under my touch, then lowers his arms to his sides as I explore the Celtic tribal design that swoops over his shoulder and down his arm. "You showed me your tattoo for a reason." When I reach the end of his tattoo on his forearm, I notice the skin along his pectoral is prickled. Loving that I'm affecting him, I step closer and slide my hand along the pattern that continues across his ribcage. "Tell me about it."

Calder brushes my hair over my shoulder and clasps the back of my neck. Rubbing his thumb just below the choker, he says, "I got the tattoo on my shoulder before I joined the Navy. It was meant to represent the Irish heritage of my family name."

I don't miss the past tense in his statement. What happened to make him distance himself from the Blake family? When he doesn't elaborate, but instead begins to massage the back of my neck, I realize he's not planning to say more, so I trace my fingers over the single word Solus on his ribs. "What does this mean?"

Calder captures my hand and lifts it between us, palm up. Pressing his lips to the inside of my fingers, he moves lower and tenderly kisses my palm, letting his lips linger. My stomach flutters and I marvel at how the merest touch of his mouth to my skin affects me so deeply.

He trails his lips to the heel of my hand, then starts to push my shirtsleeve out of the way to kiss my wrist. When he sees the bottom part of my tattoo, he pauses and shifts his gaze to mine. Our eyes lock and my heart races. I feel the tug of his fingers working the cuff's button and I react on instinct. I start to pull away, but his hold tightens on my wrist.

A half smile tugs his lips. "I knew I was right." Releasing me, he takes a step back and gestures to my shirt. "I showed you mine. Now it's your turn to show me yours."

Sharing the truth about my lack of orgasm success was painful enough, but my tattoos are incredibly and deeply personal, both for the loss they represent and the years of heart-rending self-doubt they cover up.

I don't know if I have the courage to share them with him, but when he looks at me like that—with heated want and intrigued curiosity swirling in his gaze—he gives me the courage to try. On my terms.

Instead of reaching for the buttons on my shirt, I hook my fingers on my skirt's metal button and pop it free of the thick denim. I watch Calder's Adam's apple bob as I unzip the skirt. Once I shimmy out of it, I drop the skirt and my underwear to the wood floor.

His eyebrow shoots up and his gaze darkens with lustful thoughts. I reach for the top button of my shirt, and Calder's gaze hungrily follows my nimble fingers until the last button is undone. The whole time I free the buttons, I make sure to keep the shirt closed.

Sliding my fingers along the shirt's edges, I reach for the front clasp holding my bra closed and release it.

Calder's gaze darkens even more, and when I don't immediately open my shirt, he lowers his arms and starts to take a step forward.

I hold my hand up. "Wait, Calder."

Though he's playing it cool, his chest rises and falls at a faster pace.

I start to reach for the necklace, but he jerks his head back and forth. "Everything goes but that. Don't take it off."

I love his intensity. Nodding, I trail my fingers past my neck, then push back the shirt and my bra at the same time.

Calder's gaze instantly drops to my breasts as the clothes

slide off my arms onto the floor behind me. A grin flashes. I knew where his attention would focus. I need him to stay distracted.

Except he doesn't.

Just when I let myself relax and enjoy his appreciation of my naked state, his smile fades and he steps forward. Clasping my hands, he lifts and turns them so he can inspect my tattoos.

"Does 'Never' have to do with the raven?" he asks, glancing up.

When he moves to slide his thumb across the black bird, I tug my wrists free and take a step back. "What does 'Solus' mean?"

His expression shutters and his lips twist in a wry smile, acknowledging that neither of us wants to share the pain behind our ink. "Aren't we a pair?"

Tilting my head, I spread my hands, my lips curving. "We could try being a pair togeth—" Calder steps into me and lifts me, cutting me off.

As I grasp his hard shoulders and slide down his body, he holds me aloft and captures a nipple, sucking it deep into his mouth.

I fold my legs around his body and pull him close, gasping at the pleasure his immediate possession elicits. Digging my fingers into his hair, my voice is breathy against his temple. "This might be easier lying down."

"The last word I would ever use to describe us is easy, angel," he chuckles against my breast even as he carries me toward his bed.

The bedspread is cool against my back as Calder leans over me and runs his nose along my neck, inhaling deeply. I glide my fingers into his hair and sigh my contentment of being this close to him after all this time. He smells so good, all male and strong soap.

When he lifts his dog tags off me, it makes me a little sad to lose them, but I'm too caught up in the tingling sensation of his other hand sliding along the inside of my thigh.

"Do you have any idea how hard it was not to go straight to your house that night after the party?" he says, holding my gaze. "It felt like you were blowing me off, and then I found out about my...father."

When he grips my thigh, then lowers his forehead on my shoulder, exhaling harshly, I press my fingers into the back of his neck, pulling him close. "I'm sorry about your dad, Calder. Talia told me he passed away. I can't imagine how hard that must've been."

He glances up at me, his expression haunted. "It was hard enough losing my mother when I was younger, but my father's death changed everything for me." Easing his hold on my thigh, the sadness in his tone shifts to a tender one. "You were my last pleasant memory, and right now all I want to do is drown in you."

His unintended confession breaks my heart. I want to yank him close, wrap my whole body around his hard masculine frame and tell him that I'm here for him, like he was for me. But maybe losing himself in the moment is exactly what he needs for now. This moment of intimacy with Calder is all I've dreamed about ever since that party.

When he shifts over me, I want him to know he's not alone in his need for a connection between us. I want to show him that I need it just as much, maybe even more. Before he can make the first move, I rise up on my elbows and press my mouth to his.

Calder rumbles against my mouth, his hands cupping my head as he slants his lips over mine. I sense his desperate desire for more, but the intensity I know he's capable of feels leashed somehow, like he's trying not to overwhelm me. The last thing I want him to do is hold back. Watching him intentionally antagonize his opponent tonight, coupled with the comment he made in the car about being a Blake, then just now about losing his dad...it feels like he's on an edgy, destructive path. I refuse to let him go further down that road. He needs to know that I'm the one person he'll have the freedom to be himself with.

I fist my fingers in his hair and yank slightly to get his attention before he distracts me too much. When he breaks our kiss to frown at me, I loosen my fingers. "Don't hold back on me, Calder. I want the full you, all of you...the good, the bad, and the dark side too."

Wariness reflects in his gaze before he flashes a smile. "You'll have it, angel. Every dirty inch of me."

The last thing I expect is for him to get up, but when he walks over and starts sifting through his vinyl records, I'm immediately intrigued. "That's definitely old-school..." I trail off, hoping he'll tell me about it.

He glances up as he slides a single out of its cover. His

brow furrows for a second before he says, "It was my...dad's passion. There's quite a collection at his house."

I roll over on my stomach and watch him pull more records out.

"So none of those are from your dad's collection?"

Calder turns back to the record player and answers as he changes the short center spindle for a tall one before carefully stacking the spindle several records deep. "No, these are all mine." He flashes a wicked smile. "Get ready for an eclectic mix that spans several decades."

His dog tags are still on the bed, and I lift them up while he turns on the player and tests the needle for dust.

Blake, Calder J.

An old blues song starts to play. When a woman's amazing voice belts the drawn out word "Fever" in an awesome introduction to the seductive tone of the song, I raise my eyebrows and grin.

"Shirley Horn," Calder supplies the singer's name before walking into his kitchen. "Do you want anything to drink?"

I shake my head and stare at the dog tags once more. "What does the 'J' stand for?" I ask, rubbing my fingers over the name.

Calder approaches, drinking ice water. Setting the empty glass down on his nightstand, he sits beside me and slides my hair over my shoulder, then trails his knuckles down my back. "I'll tell you mine if you tell me yours."

I snicker, then realize he's serious. "You really aren't going to tell me?"

He shakes his head as he skims his fingers over the curve of my butt. "Nope."

I hesitate, but it's not like I'm telling him who I am by giving a middle name. "It's Nadia."

Interest flickers in his green gaze. "Is your family of Slavic origin?"

Oh, he's good, trying to weasel information out of me. I shake my head. "No. My mom just liked the name. Your turn."

He takes the dog tags and drops them on top of the ice in the glass. "It's Jackson."

"I didn't realize tags needed to be put on ice," I tease.

He tugs on my shoulder, rolling me onto my back. Sliding his palm between my breasts, he leans over and kisses my nose, then my cheek, then my throat, saying in a husky tone, "They've been against your hot body all night. Of course they need a cooling down period."

I arch my back when he cups my breast fully. Sliding my fingers down his hard chest, I trail them down his cut abs. "Wouldn't they be just as hot against your skin?"

Just when my fingers reach the waistband of his pants, he slides off the bed, his strong hands clasping my hips and turning me with him. Pulling me to the edge of the bed, he commands in a suddenly intense tone, "Hook your legs over my shoulders."

I immediately do as he asks, my heart rate elevating. As he presses a cool kiss to my inner thigh, chill bumps break out on my skin. I bite my bottom lip in anticipation and slide my hands over his corded forearms, enjoying the movement of muscle under my fingers.

"You have no idea how many times I've relived that time with you," he rasps, his breath growing warmer as he skims past my entrance to press a slow lingering kiss much lower on my other thigh.

I clench his arms tight and try to inch closer, breathing out, "Not nearly as many times as I have."

He kisses the bit of hair at the top of my mound, then moves to the left and plants a lingering kiss on the crease of my leg. When he suddenly clamps down on the sensitive tendon, I jump. My fingers digging into his arms, my heart pounds out of control and I instinctively pull my thighs inward.

But Calder doesn't let go. I hear his breathing elevating and feel the harsh bursts of warm breath rushing against my sensitive skin. His hands slide up the back of my thighs and when he reaches mid-way, he slowly pulls my thighs open once more.

I'm panting, and my body is throbbing with want, while my uncertainty of what's coming next, coupled with my worry that I'll fail to climax, is keeping me from relaxing. Calder slides a hand to my belly and flattens it against my heaving abs. His hand is warm and large, easily covering most of my stomach.

When he applies pressure and glances up at me, I see the lust in his gaze, but also the tender command. *Settle, I'm here.*

I take several breaths and force myself to relax. When my breath stops heaving, he returns his hand to the back of my thigh. The moment he loosens his bite on my body and then releases me, a sudden rush of lust rolls from my belly to my sex in a heavy seductive pull. Surprised, I moan and flex my inner muscles, my hips rolling without conscious thought or effort.

Calder slides his thumbs down my thighs, bringing his fingers together at my center. I tingle with a pleasant sting as he spreads my sensitive lips wide and stares, but the pleasure deepens when I see the passionate heat in his expression. I feel its intensity all the way to my toes.

"I love seeing how much you want this. You're soaked with milky sweetness and it's fucking gorgeous." His gaze darkens, full of ravenous intent. "Are you ready to be reminded there's no such thing as a fluke when it comes to us?"

Calder doesn't wait for me to say "yes", instead just as the record changes to a slow, seductive beat with deep bluesy undertones and the woman's sexy voice tells the guy, "I Put a Spell on You," he leans forward and murmurs, "Nina Simone got it so fucking right," just before he slowly slides his tongue deep inside me.

CHAPTER TWENTY

CALDER

*F*uck, she tastes like heaven. Her warm, sweet flavor clings to my tongue, and I swallow greedily, then dive in for more, devouring her gorgeous body. I bite and suck and possess every delicious inch of her sweet pussy, loving the pressure of her legs tightening around my shoulders, the arch of her back, and my necklace standing out against the graceful curve of her neck. It looks so damn hot on her.

The moment I pulled her in front of the mirror, I felt a knee-dropping punch in the gut. It was one thing to imagine my gift on her, but another entirely to see it around her neck.

Raven's hand slides into my hair and fists tight, pulling me fully into the moment. When she arches and rolls her hips, exhaling my name between gasps of passion, my cock grows ten times harder. "Show me what you've got, angel.

P. T. MICHELLE

Let it build and give it to me," I rumble against her before sucking her clit hard. As a shudder rocks through her, I throb with the need to bury myself inside her, but I ignore the yearning building in my stomach and the tightening of my balls. I want her to enjoy this ecstasy.

It's mine too in a way; I definitely derive my own sense of pleasure from it. As I watch her passion build, I feel invincible. I refuse to think about the pathetic motherfuckers who came before me. Those assholes who didn't know how to get her off don't exist as far as I'm concerned. One thing's for sure, I'm the unrelenting bastard she'll never say that about. If anything, before the evening is done, she'll be begging me for a break.

She's the woman I crave, the one I lie awake at night thinking about. The one whose face I've seen on the few one-night-stands I've had these last four years. I want her, even if I don't deserve her. But I also want to really know her, starting with her name. I screwed up my chance to find out on my own years ago. I was too damned lost in my own misery, but she makes me forget about that stuff. I never thought about how important a first name is...until she refused to give me hers, and it's driving me fucking nuts.

I understand giving one's word, but what's happening between us...the deep intensity should count for something. I want to know what she does for a living. Did she follow her dreams? What do her tattoos mean and why won't she let me touch them? And why the hell is she willingly pretending to be someone else?

I'm so frustrated that I know so little about her that my

hands instinctively grip her perfect ass tight. I know it's primitive...this need to show her we're still deeply connected after all this time, but I won't let her leave before she believes that, because once she does, she'll trust me enough to share.

I tilt her hips and press my face against her soft skin, inhaling her, soaking in her sweetness. I want her achy and desperate, those hips moving so fast, seeking the kind of satisfied release only I can give her. With wicked ruthlessness, I nip at her pussy lips and watch her squirm and writhe. Fuck, I love every second of testing her limits.

I need to know how much she can take before I finally slide inside her, because once I make that final step with her, I won't be able to hold back. She jacks me up too much. I *will* fuck her boneless and revel in her cries of bliss and my own tightening pleasure as her hot, wet body sucks me dry. I can't wait to inhale near her neck and clasp her close so I can feel her yield fully against me. She has her own special scent of herbal shampoo and other womanly smells I've yet to decipher, but they're specific enough that once I'm not jacked up with the need to bury my dick as deep into her as humanly possible, I'll parse them out and break every bit of her down.

With my head swimming in her gasps of pleasure, I ease back and slide two fingers deep inside her. I want to watch her come apart this time, to see her lush breasts bounce with her ragged breaths and rocking hips. I ruthlessly press deeper, and once I find those tiny little ridges, I stroke the hell out of her g-spot, taking her to a new heightened level of pleasure.

When Raven explodes against my hand, watching her body shudder and her cheeks flush with her exertions is so arousing, I apply pressure on her clit with my thumb and keep my fingers moving inside her. I draw her orgasm out as long as possible, for my own perverse pleasure.

The back of my neck tenses and my stomach tightens before I realize that my chest is heaving and I'm about to lose it. *How the fuck did my hips get pressed against the bed?* Gritting my teeth, I jerk my dick away from the mattress edge, eliminating the temptation to rub one out. She's so fucking sexy to watch that I completely lost myself in the mesmerizing moment.

Taking several deep breaths, I glide my wet fingers into my mouth and watch her come down from her high. She's the picture of wanton abandon: her arms thrown over her head, pink nipples rising and falling with her erratic breaths, skin glowing. She looks like a very satisfied beautiful angel. *My angel.*

I stand and lean over her, kissing her panting lips, sharing in her post-orgasmic bliss. "Not a fluke, gorgeous."

CHAPTER TWENTY-ONE

CASS

I feel like a boneless kitten when Calder crawls into bed and settles me in front of him, tucking my back into his warm chest. Though I'm surprised he's still wearing his pants, I'm too blissfully content to protest. That was the best oral sex I've ever had in my life, even better than four years ago. The man has a magical mouth, tongue, and hands. Everything about him turns me on.

While he folds his muscular arm around my waist, I rest my head on his pillow and wait for my heart to settle back to a less crazed pace.

When Calder's hand slides to my breast and his thumb slowly strokes my nipple as he presses his lips to my neck, I lift my arm behind me and bury my fingers in his thick hair, pulling him closer.

Calder clasps my hand and kisses my fingers, then sucks each one before pressing his lips to the raven on my wrist.

I tense and start to pull away, but his hold on my hand tightens. "What does the raven mean to you?"

I close my eyes and exhale slowly, then blink as a new song starts up. This one is more recent. Chris Isaak's "Wicked Game" is slow and tortured, exactly how the words feel as I tell him about my sister taking her life to save our father from an impossible task of prolonging hers. "Sophie was the fun one, the positive vibe in our house. Losing her left a deep hole in our family that has never really been filled. The night before she..."

When I pause and take a deep breath, Calder kisses my temple, the simple gesture telling me that he's sorry I lost my sister. His compassion gives me the strength to keep talking. "She told me her wish was to come back as a raven so she can travel the world." I pull my arm free and stare at the tattoo. "I got this to always keep her memory with me. So far she's seen quite a bit, at least a dozen countries."

"So you fulfilled your dream of traveling the world. Did you do it by creating imagery that takes everyone's breath away?"

Nodding, I blink hard and try not to get choked up that he remembered what I'd said to him that night we exchanged notes. "I did. Pick up back issues of Vogue and Harper's Bazaar and you'll see some of my work."

"Ah, I see...photography," he says as he laces his fingers with mine.

I twist the hand he's holding, turning my raven tattoo upward once more. "Photography credit goes to Raven, so you see, my sister's fulfilling all kinds of dreams."

Turning our locked fingers, he rubs his thumb along the script on my forearm. "And this one? What does it represent?"

"It just means to 'never give up.'" I don't want him prying too deeply about my tattoos. I'm thankful he hasn't noticed the scars yet, so I roll to face him and trace my fingers over the word on his side. "Your turn. What does Solus mean?"

Calder tucks a strand of hair behind my ear. "It means 'alone.'"

The meaning behind his tattoo makes my heart break. I cup my hand over the word on his skin and meet his gaze. "But you don't have to be, Calder."

Spearing his fingers in my hair, he sets his forehead against mine. "I do right now, angel."

I squeeze his muscle underneath my hand. "If it's a temporary thing, why did you permanently ink it to your skin?"

Calder sighs, then runs his nose along my cheek. "The EUC is too dangerous for you to be around. Do not go to the rescheduled fight with Beth."

I notice he didn't answer my question, but his response makes me pull back and frown. "If it's so dangerous, why aren't you worried about Beth?"

He jams his hand into his hair and rolls over on his back, pulling me with him. "Because she's dating one of the guys running the outfit. I've seen her disappear with some of the security guards at past events."

"Just like she did tonight," I muse aloud. When he nods,

I lean on his chest. "There's no way Beth knows. I can't see her being willingly involved with dangerous criminals."

"Well, she is." He looks at me and shrugs. "I have no idea how much she knows about their strong-arm business practices."

"Strong-arm?" I lean on his chest, tension vibrating through me. "Are you being coerced into fighting? Is that why you're doing this, Calder? We should call the police."

He shakes his head and folds his hand over mine resting on his chest. "No, I'm not being coerced, but a family friend was hurt. They put Gil in the hospital for asking too many questions about one of the guys who trained at his gym. Thomas was a promising MMA fighter who disappeared this year after he refused to take a bribe to throw a EUC fight."

"I remember the announcer mentioning a guy named Rampage dropping out of the event. Was that Thomas?"

Calder nods. "He didn't drop out. He disappeared. I'd been sparring and grappling with him for a while and knew his techniques, so when Gil ended up in the hospital, I amped my game to get the EUC's attention."

I wrap my arm around his trim waist and squeeze. "You're doing this to find out what happened to Thomas?"

He nods. "In case you're wondering...I would never fucking throw a fight. Thankfully I haven't been asked to. But beyond learning about Thomas, my goal is to put EUC out of business before they can hurt the New York MMA fighters' chance of getting approved to go pro. It's time New York stopped holding out approval. If they'd just legitimize the sport, this kind of underground shit couldn't get the traction it does. There would be regulators and a lot of cameras watching every aspect."

Sliding his hand along my jaw, he traces his thumb across my cheekbone. "That's why I let my friendship with Celeste continue. While I was standing outside the Carver estate talking to Celeste that day I went to apologize to her, I saw Beth get into her car and drive off."

"You recognized Beth from the EUC?" I ask, folding my hand over his.

"Instantly. I tried sneaking a look at Beth's contacts over her shoulder while she scrolled through her phone to put my number in it at the party today. I'd hoped I could discover one of the guys behind EUC. The fighters never interact with management. They only ever see the security hired to run the events. That same security are also the ones who give us our cash payments after each bout. Unfortunately, Beth moved too fast, so I couldn't see any names."

"I know her boyfriend's first name is Brent, but that's all she said about him," I tell him. "I didn't even know she was dating anyone until we went to the fight tonight. I could try to find out more."

"No." Calder's expression turns fierce. "I don't want you to do anything. Stay away from this, Raven. Understood?"

I drop my gaze to his chest and trace my finger across his hard pectoral. "I'll make a deal with you. I won't get involved if you promise to call Sebastian. Talia says he's worried about you."

"She said something similar to me at the christening," Calder snorts. "Man, she's starting to sound like his wife."

My gaze snaps to his. "Um, maybe that's because she is."

Calder's eyes cloud over and hurt reflects briefly in his gaze before he shutters it. "They got married?"

I nod. "Don't feel too bad. I wasn't invited either. They quietly tied the knot. I've suggested they have a party to make it up to those of us who feel slighted for being left out of such an important day in their lives."

"It's his life," Calder says with a shrug. "It's not a choice I plan to make, but I wish him well."

"You don't believe in marriage?" I pose the question with my lips curved in amusement to hide the fact that my stomach suddenly feels like it's sinking.

Calder pulls me fully on top of him until his mouth is almost touching mine. "You don't have to have a piece of paper to have passion that doesn't fade with time. We've proven that."

In an instant, I'm flipped completely over on top of him. As I face the ceiling, he cups my breasts and kisses a path along my neck. I put my feet on the bed and arch into his hands, loving how he possesses me with cocky boldness. Calder doesn't take the slow approach. Sex with him is instantly fierce, full of eroticism that burns white-hot. The moment an unbidden moan escapes my lips, he plops his pillows on my belly and rolls us both over.

"Lift your hips, angel," he husks while grabbing the edges of the pillows under me.

When I push up slightly on my knees, he doubles the

pillows over, elevating my hips even higher. I start to lift up on my hands, but he bends over my back, his warm chest completely covering mine. Taking my hands, he stretches them fully forward, commanding, "Leave them here and don't move."

My heart races, but I hold this incredibly vulnerable position, trusting him completely. I jump when a piece of ice slowly glides along my spine. "You have such a beautiful body," he murmurs right before he nips at my right hip. When I gasp and arch, enthralled by this primitive side to him, he cups the ice over the sting, then moves his mouth to press a tender kiss to my left butt cheek.

I relax into the soft kiss, only to jerk once more when he bites down on the round flesh. *That'll definitely leave a mark.* The moment he releases me, my body is already reacting to his erotic branding. A flood of sheer want pools between my legs, the throbbing sensation making me grind against the pillows.

Calder grabs my hips and lifts me back up. "Not yet, angel. I'm just getting started." He chuckles darkly when the song "Need you Tonight" by INXS begins to thump seductively through the room.

The pulsing base in the music isn't freaking helping my situation. "Put your mouth on me, Calder," I beg, my fingers digging into the edge of the mattress.

He leans across my back, his hard muscles flexing against me. Just as he whispers in my ear, "I plan to," he cups his hand firmly on my sex.

I squeal at the ice he's holding against me and try to

squirm away, but his powerful thighs and bigger body have me pinned. All I can do is pant and shiver...and want.

Just when I think I can't stand it any longer, he lifts his body off me. I barely have a chance to miss his amazing smell and the warmth of his skin against mine before he grabs my ass and thrusts his hot tongue deep into my cold entrance. Moaning, I press shamelessly against him, loving the sensation of his groans of approval vibrating against me. Calder presses deep, sucking my juices at the same time he slides a hand under me to rub my clit.

I rock my hips and mewl against the bed, my breathing jacking.

He's relentless in his technique with the ice. He touches different parts of my body with ice, then warms it with his hot mouth, ramping the intensity between us. Each time is the same, yet different enough to make me yelp again and again until my thighs are shaking and I'm sure I'm going to lose my mind.

"Just fuck me," I demand, sounding like a woman possessed.

When Calder slides two fingers inside me, and I let out a moan of pleasure, tightening my body around them, he rasps, "Is this enough, angel?"

I buck back against him, needing release, but he just holds his hand still as he places his other hand on the bed beside me and leans close. "See how that's just a tease, how it only feels half as good as it could? I'm not going to fuck your beautiful pussy without knowing your name."

"What?" I tense and jerk my gaze to his. "Are you serious?"

His face hardens, his hips pressing against mine. "Very. You want me? You're going to have to give it up, baby."

"You said you would wait." I attempt to negotiate while his fingers are still buried inside me.

His eyes darken and he pushes deeper, turning his hand and rubbing on that spot that drives me nuts. "The thing about giving your word, sweet Raven, it should only be as strong as your trust in the person you give it to. When I come inside you, I want it as real as it gets, which should start with knowing your goddamn name."

I turn away, blinking back tears. I want it to be as-real-as-it-gets too. So much. Celeste and her stupid, fucking ultimatums.

Calder moves his hips, pressing his erection against my butt, which forces his hand deeper inside me. I moan and counter, rocking my hips. *When did he take off his pants?* God, he had me so wrapped up, I didn't even notice, but the sensation of his engorged cock so close is driving me crazy. I roll my hips in a seductive move that takes full advantage of him pressing against me.

"Fucking hell," he mutters, yanking his hips back. Breathing heavily, he demands, "At least tell me your first name, damn it!"

I squeeze my eyes shut. I've done everything Celeste asked. Went above and beyond.

"Angel, please...trust me." Calder lays fully on top of me,

his hard body tense, hips pinning me still. Sliding his hands along my wrists, he twines our fingers together. His hold tight, he whispers in my ear, "There's nothing I want more than to fuck your sweet pussy into the most satisfying release."

I feel empty without him touching me between my legs. My body craves the ultimate connection he's promising. Only with him. My trust in Calder is instinctual and strong. Far more than anyone else. He has my trust. "It's Cass Rockwell," I breathe out, feeling a twinge of guilt for not keeping my word. But he's wrong about one thing...it's not always about whether the recipient deserves it. Sometimes your word is all you have, and without it you're nothing. I know that better than anyone.

"Cass," Calder murmurs, testing my name out and drawing me back under his spell. Kissing my shoulder, he says it once more as he eases back.

When the head of his cock slips inside my entrance and he slowly pushes forward, I let out a soft cry of want, then freeze. "Condom?"

"Always," he confirms as he slides a hand down my back. Anchoring his other hand on my hip, he tenses, pausing his forward movement. "Christ, if you don't let go of that grip a little, Cass, we're not going to make it past round one."

I take a deep breath and try to relax.

"That's my girl." He presses deeper, then grits out, "Fuck...I can't..." right before he rams deep.

When I yelp, he clasps my hips and stills. "Are you okay?"

I nod and flex around his thickness, letting him know I'm fine.

"Don't do that. Not yet," he says before he slowly exhales and his hands tighten on my hips

He's still not moving and that's all I want to do, but I force myself to remain perfectly still and wait for him to make the first move.

Several calming breaths later, Calder pulls almost completely out of me and eases halfway back inside.

My belly flutters and I rock my hips, my actions rubbing the tip of his cock along an amazing pleasure center. Calder lets out a low, wicked chuckle and lifts up higher, then applies pressure with counter thrusts.

Skin tingling, I pant and babble out incoherent gasps among chants of his name and pleas for more.

He grips my pelvis and tilts me, arching my back. Whenever I move, I'm in pre-orgasmic heaven. Shaking and quivering all over, I'm just on the edge. And I can't believe now is when I realize I haven't felt the darkness that normally surrounds me during sex. Calder is so distracting, so consuming, I don't have time to think. Just feel...and it's so amazing I never want it to end.

Bending close, he slides his hand along my belly until he reaches my clit. Stroking with a knowing touch, he demands in his low bass, "Come, Cass. Give me the best damn orgasm, angel."

He tweaks my clit once more and I tumble over the edge

as fiery passion flares through me. Clawing at the sheets, I jut back against Calder, grinding on his cock like a cat in heat. The sounds of his breathing spiking and his knowing hands moving over me while my own pulse *whooshes* in my ears only adds to my feverish climax.

The second my gasps slow, Calder begins to move in and out of me in steadily harder strokes. My body reacts to his erotic rhythm and hard friction, my core soaking once more, building for another release.

When I lift up on my hands to better counter his movements, Calder leans over and pulls me to my knees like him. Wrapping an arm around my waist, he nudges us forward, gruffly commanding, "Use the headboard for leverage."

As soon as I grip the smooth, curved wood, I cry out in shock when Calder lowers his dog tags over my head. I instantly shiver at the ice-frigid metal beads searing into my flushed skin and his tags resting between my breasts. The contrast is so arousing, I clench Calder hard enough to draw a pained grunt. Gripping my waist, he jerks his hips forward, burrowing deeper and growling his own fierce response. I gasp at the fullness possessing my body and press back against him, loving his aggressiveness.

Calder's movements are so hard and fierce, I pant in building excitement, each time feeling like a deeper possession. Before I realize it, my breasts are pressed against the headboard and the rhythmic rubbing of my nipples against the polished wood, combined with the cool metal against my skin, hikes my adrenaline to a fever pitch.

As a powerful orgasm rips a scream from me, Calder

rams deep once more, then groans through his own release. We're both still panting when he captures my neck and hauls me back against his hard chest, the fine sheen of sweat between us fusing our bodies even more. Feathering his fingers down my throat, he touches the edge of the choker and rumbles against my jaw, "Now you're fully mine."

CHAPTER TWENTY-TWO

CASS

*W*e stay in that position for a while, our fast breathing the only sound in the quiet room. As if on cue, even the records had stopped playing. Calder presses a kiss to my shoulder then whispers against my throat, "I'll never get enough."

I'm surprised to feel him hardening inside me once more. It makes me giddy in an exhausted kind of way. I lift his hand and kiss his palm. "Let me catch my breath."

He chuckles in my ear and while he heads for the bathroom, I lie down on his pillow and soak in his wonderful smell.

Calder turns off the lights and climbs into bed behind me, his strong arm sliding me fully against his chest. I settle into the protective cradle of his muscular body and bask in the blissfully content feeling.

He brushes my hair behind my ear and says, "What does Celeste get out of this?"

It's not that I don't trust him to keep this between us, but I've already broken my own word. He has no idea how much it feels like I've betrayed myself. It's not him, it's me dealing with my own issues. "Celeste's reasons are her own to tell, Calder." I close my eyes, my stomach tightening. I can't shake the feeling that I've failed and all of this is going to blow up in my face.

He exhales his frustration against the back of my neck, his fingers stroking through my hair. "Don't go back. Whatever it is...blow it off."

I roll to face him and kiss his jaw. "It's not that simple. This isn't just about me. Celeste has the ability to help my dad get a project approved. It's something that he's been trying to do for years without success."

"Do you think Celeste would give you as much loyalty as you're giving her right now?"

Sounds like he knows Celeste pretty well, but this is about seeing my word through, at least the part of it I kept. "I can't say."

When his expression hardens, I cup my hand on his jaw. "Would you not fight if I asked you to?"

His jaw flexes under my palm. "That's different."

"No, it's not."

Digging his fingers into my hair, his eyes glitter in the darkness. "The difference is you know the whole story. I don't."

I move my hand to the Solus word on his ribcage. "Do I?"

"That has nothing to do with my fighting." He holds my gaze for a beat before he continues, "I feel like there's a lot more that you're not telling me." Clasping my wrist, he starts to lift my hand to his mouth, then pauses, his brow furrowing as he slowly draws his thumb across the scars.

Before our gazes can lock once more, I roll back over and mumble, "I don't know for sure what she's doing, Calder." I can guess...and it's sad and truthfully none of my business.

"Forget about Celeste." He slides his hand down my arm, reaching for my wrist. "Cass—"

"Just hold me, Calder," I say, threading my fingers with his.

He doesn't say another word. He just pulls me close and whispers in my ear, "You're mine now. I'll always keep you safe."

As Calder's muscular arm around my waist grows heavier in his sleep, I revel in the feeling of comfort his last words bring to my heart. I want to tell him why sticking to my word means so much to me, but it's too mired in a past I don't want to dredge up. Just thinking about that day fills me with a sense of shame. No, it's not something I want to share.

But no matter how hard I try to keep the memory at bay it rushes forth anyway, a reminder that life is both precious and precarious and we should never take it for granted.

I drunkenly stumble into my dorm room in my clubbing

heels, skimpy skirt and leather jacket, thankful my roommate is with her boyfriend tonight. I'd run the three blocks from the club back to the dorm in sheer panic. I kick off the sky-high heels; that isn't the pain I desperately crave. I need something more. I have to feel what I've worked so hard to overcome. Therapy, meds, hypnosis...I'd done it all in an effort to break the cycle, and I've been good my entire freshman year. Even got my very first tattoos across my wrists as a reward to myself.

I head for the bathroom and fall to my knees, digging for my makeup bag. I rip open the zipper on the cloth bag and makeup flies everywhere. I peel back the compartment inside where I'd hidden a blade and hold it aloft.

I'm so screwed up. I'll never be normal. Never have a fucking real relationship.

I can't bring myself to cut on the wrist with the raven; it was my favored wrist in the past. I shift the blade to my other hand and slide it across the opposite wrist, then lean back against the bathroom door as the pain and sheer bliss wash over me.

Several seconds pass as I revel in the most euphoric state I've ever experienced. I close my eyes and vaguely wonder if it feels so good because it's been so long.

Then Sophie's voice is whispering in my ear. "What are you doing? You promised, Cass. You gave me your word you would help Dad! You can't go back on that. Open your eyes!"

She's so upset, so distraught it sounds like she's right here in the bathroom with me. My eyes fly open and I glance around the tiny bathroom. "Sophie?"

My knees slip on the floor as I swivel around, looking for my sister. Why is the floor wet? It feels like things move in slow motion once I look down and see the pool of blood under me.

I blink in confusion before it hits me that I cut too deep. Wooziness floods my mind, making me lightheaded. "You gave me your word!" *Sophie calls in my ear once more.*

"I know," *I whisper through the tears streaking down my cheeks.*

My arms feel like noodles, but I manage to grab a towel and wrap it tight around my wrist.

Crawling to my purse feels like I'm swimming through molasses, but I finally pull out my phone and dial 911.

"911. What's the state of your emergency?" *the operator says in a clipped tone.*

"I—I think I need an ambulance," *I croak out.*

"What is your name?" *she asks.*

I blink and clasp my wrist tighter against my chest.

"Stay on the line. Can you tell me what's wrong?"

"Too much blood," *is all I manage to say before darkness overtakes me.*

Coming back to the present, I sigh in the darkness. After I woke in the hospital, they put me on suicide watch for a while, until they were convinced I wasn't a danger to myself any longer.

Almost dying—even by accident—was the wakeup call I needed to get my shit together. If it hadn't been for Sophie— well, my mind conjuring my sister's voice reminding me to keep my word—I wouldn't be here today.

I lift Calder's hand and press a kiss to his knuckles. He mumbles in his sleep and pulls me closer. I smile in the darkness and let myself fully relax in his warm embrace.

I AWAKE WITH A START, blinking in the dark room. Calder's arm is tight around my waist, his breathing even in deep sleep.

The ceiling illuminates across the room, drawing my attention. It's my phone. I glance at Calder's nightstand clock. *Oh, shit, it's one a.m.* As gently as I can, I ease out of the bed so I don't wake him. He rolls over, but remains fast asleep.

When I reach the phone I can see that I have a missed call from Beth. I try to tap the notification, hoping it'll let me in, but the lock screen pops up for a code.

What four number code would Celeste possibly put in for me? As I stare at the keypad, the letters jump out at me. Could it be that simple?

I quickly type in 2277 for my name. When the lock screen disappears, I breathe a sigh of relief, then tap on the voice message icon.

"Celeste, where the hell are you? Dad called me freaking out. Must be all the kiss-ass crap he's got lined up for us to host this week. Get your butt home right now. I don't want to have to deal with him alone. I'm on my way as well."

I immediately text Celeste.

Where are you? It's an hour past when you said you'd be home.

Five minutes later, I type another text.

Should I go back to your house and wait for you to call me tomorrow morning?

I wait another ten minutes, then walk into Calder's bathroom and dial a taxi service, trying not to panic. Where is Celeste? Why isn't she answering my texts?

Once I'm dressed, I walk over and stare at Calder sleeping soundly under the moonlight shining through the big window. He's sprawled on his back in the big bed, muscular arms resting above his head and powerful thighs tangled in his white sheets. Even relaxed in sleep, his fit body looks like a warrior's with his Celtic tribal tattoo standing in contrast against the stark sheets.

We'd fallen asleep with no more words said, but it was still a comforting silence. I hate that I have to leave like a thief in the night, but if I wake him up, he'll just try to convince me to stay. I force myself to look away before I lean over and kiss him awake.

Reaching up, I try to remove the choker he gave me, but I can't quite get the clasp to work. My finger hooks on a small ring, so I use the ring to pull it forward and work the clasp while looking in the bathroom mirror.

Laying the necklace and his dog tags next to the turntable, I slip the note I wrote him under them.

CALDER,

. . .

I'm sorry I have to leave my choker. While it's badass and totally something I would wear, the style isn't Celeste's. I'm leaving it here in your safe-keeping.

CASS

RAVEN089276@BOXMAIL.COM

As THE TAXI pulls into the drive, I see two men standing in the driveway beside an unmarked police car. They're talking to Celeste's father, who'd slipped on a pair of jeans and a sweater. Before I even get out of the car, Phillip appears around the side of the Carver's home, tugging on a zip-up pullover. Apparently he'd walked over from his estate. It's not a good sign if Gregory called his lawyer. Unfortunately it's too late to ask the driver to pull away.

Taking a breath, I pay the taxi and get out. "What's going on?" I say as the taxi pulls away.

Gregory gestures to me, obvious relief on his face. "See detectives, my daughter is safe and sound. I knew there was some kind of horrible mistake."

"I told you she was with me," Beth grumbles, arms folded. She's ticked I ruined her night out with Brent.

"We'll discuss why she's arriving separately later, young lady," Gregory reprimands Beth before he walks over to stand beside me. "We're just glad you're home safe, Celeste."

I wrap my arms around myself to ward off the late night chill in the air and ask, "Why did you think I wasn't safe?"

The reed-thin detective holding an old-school notepad and pen glances my way, his dark eyebrows hiked. "We're glad to see you're okay, Miss Carver. We found an abandoned rental car on a stretch of 495 with your ID in the floorboard and blood coating the seat and driver's-side door. We'll be testing the blood, but in the meantime, can you tell us how your ID ended up in a rental car?"

Oh shit...has something happened to Celeste? I swallow the bile rising in my throat and dart my gaze between the detectives, Phillip, Gregory, and Beth.

CHAPTER TWENTY-THREE

CALDER

*G*il tugs his golfer's cap down over his curly salt-and-pepper hair, then gestures with his cane from his position on the stool against the cinder block wall. "Your turn, Zeke. Hop on the mat. Calder, get on there and show 'em how it's done, son."

Gil's lined face looks tired. I want to tell him to go home, that I'll coach the guys, but he's determined to get his mojo back, so I keep my mouth shut.

Zeke bounds over to the mat, pulling on fighter gloves. With a stock of thick, dirty-blond hair and dark, almost black eyes, he can't be more than eighteen, but he's lean and hungry. And fucking fast. I watched him kickboxing with the bag earlier. Still, he's green and cocky as hell.

The poor kid doesn't have a chance. I don't even have to take him to the floor to best him. A few punches, some body locks and one good choke-hold shakes him up, before a powerful kick to his neck lands him to the mat and finishes him off.

I help him up and pat his shoulder. "Remember, always keep your guard up. If I'd put more force behind that hit, it would've knocked you completely out."

Nodding, he mumbles, "I guess I should be training more. I'll start coming in on Tuesdays and Thursdays too."

Gil taps his cane on the floor in approval. "Who's next?"

"I'll challenge him," a familiar voice calls through the guys crowding around to watch.

I jerk my head around as the boys part to let my cousin through, and lock gazes with Bash's bright blue one. He's standing there in slacks and a dress shirt, not a strand of his short cropped black hair out of place. The last time I saw him was over three months ago. *How the fuck did he find me?*

I turn to Gil and say, "Can you give us five?"

"No problem. Come on boys, it's nice out today. Laps for the lot of ya."

Once the grumbling men leave, I walk over to the punching bag and start with a few jabs per every step, then a one-two combo. "What are you doing here, Bash?"

"What. The. Fuck. Calder!"

I throw an extra hard left that sends the heavy bag swinging before I turn and grab a pair of gloves from the box by the wall. "You want to talk, you'll have to do it while I'm training," I snap, throwing the gloves at his chest.

Bash instantly snags the set before they fall to the floor. Tucking them under his arm, he rolls back his sleeves, muttering, "If you want a good beat down, I'm happy to oblige."

I flash a smile. "Bite me. We'll see who gets wiped first."

Bash takes off his shoes and socks, then pulls on the gloves as he meets me over on the mat.

We circle the mat, each looking for the other's weak spot. Mine just left me high and dry early this morning. Guess that means I'm back to being invincible once more.

"Is this what you're doing with your time? MMA fighting?" Bash snarls as he feigns left, then slams my shoulder with a hard right jab.

"Lucky shot," I say, just before I hammer him with a round of punches and kicks so fast he only manages to fend off about half of them.

My last punch to his chest sends a loud *oouf* rushing past his lips. I step back and bounce on the balls of my feet, hoping to rile him. "I think you might need to brush up on your training."

Bash narrows his gaze and moves like he's swinging for my ribs, but at the last second whirls into a back punch that hits me square in the chest, knocking me back.

I growl my rage and rush at him. While we've got each other trapped in different holds—he's got me in a choke-hold and I'm holding his hip and hammering at his ribs, he grates out, "This is bullshit, Cald. Why the fuck are you freezing your family out?"

I break his hold and shove him back. *"Family?* What a fucking joke."

Bash hits me with a deadly glare right before he steps forward and crosses with a fast right, clipping my jaw.

Pain explodes in my head, matching the ache that's been in my chest for four years now. His personal assault on my face sends me over the edge, and I go after him with all I've got.

I don't even remember how it happened, but for the next minute or so we beat the living shit out of each other before we end up on the mat, each of us pinning the other in a painful hold. Gritting his teeth, Bash uses his extra couple inches in height to extend his arm bar on me to the very edge of my tolerance. It hurts like a motherfucker, so I finally tap out.

Rolling to my back, I wince at the pain in my shoulder and my screaming ribs and take several deep breaths.

Panting, Bash lifts up on his elbow and looks at me, sweat rolling down his temple. "You were way fucking out of line with that family crack, Cald. What the hell is wrong with you?"

I fold my arms behind my head and stare at the gym's ceiling lights. "Do you know what I got when I finally came home after leaving the military? A letter from my mom's lawyer, telling me I'm not Jack Blake's son."

"What? That has to be bullshit."

I shrug away the defensive anger in his comment and continue to stare at the ceiling. It's easier than seeing the denial change to grudging acknowledgement in his eyes. "In the letter my mom tells me that her lawyer was given specific instructions to only deliver the notice to me if Jack passed away. The Blake last name isn't mine. That house isn't mine. Jack isn't my...father." I pause and swallow the pain of saying that last statement out loud. "And the only person I truly belonged to was so unhappy, she took her own life."

"Suicide? But you told me your mother died of a brain aneurism."

I slide my gaze his way. "It was easier on the family for that to be the official ruling." When his brow puckers, I shift my attention to the ceiling once more and start to count the stains. *Do I even fucking want to know what caused those marks up there?*

"Why did your mother tell you after all this time?"

I snort. "That's the kicker. She wanted me to know for medical reasons. So if I needed a kidney or bone marrow down the road, I could go tap dear-old-mother-fucking Dad on the shoulder and ask him for help."

Bash sits up and pulls off the gloves. Hooking his elbow on his bent knee, he stares down at me. "So did she cheat on Jack?"

I sigh and sit up too. Pulling off my gloves, I toss them down and start to unwind the tape from around my hand. "All she said was, she didn't tell my father—Jack—about 'the incident' because it would've killed him. Apparently, in the end the guilt is what killed her." I yank at the tape, tearing it off my hand with a vengeance, then tear at the tape on my other hand. "When I was a kid, I was so angry at my mom for leaving me. I saw her suicide as a betrayal of her love. She promised she'd always be there for me and she fucking took her own life, Bash. That was hard enough, but this..." I shred the rest of the damn tape and toss it down, gritting out. "It's like Jack died *twice*."

When he rests a hand on my shoulder, I finally meet his gaze. "Do you know what the most ironic thing is? I spent all our youth together making sure *you* were treated like a legitimate part of the family—because in my mind you were—when I was the one who didn't have an *ounce* of Blake blood in me. Not one fucking drop, Sebastian!"

Bash grips the back of my neck hard, his tone menacing. "If you say you're not a Blake one more fucking time, I'm going to kick your ass again. You and Jack are the ones who taught me that parents and blood don't matter, only the relationship does. Don't turn your back on your family, on *me*, fucking ever again, Cald. I love you like a brother, and it pains me to see you so tortured over such bullshit. Of all people, I know this better than anyone."

My mouth twitches with a smirk even as deep emotion rolls through my chest, lifting a bit of the heavy weight. "You've never said that before."

He claps the back of my neck hard, flashing a brilliant smile. "Talia taught me not to hold back. And now I'm telling you. Be the man your father raised you to be, the brother I know you are, who puts family above all others."

When I exhale a deep breath and say, "I'll try to remember that," he nods and leans back on his hands. "Now tell me why you're really mucking around with this MMA stuff."

"I really do enjoy it."

When his gaze narrows, I throw my hands up. "It's definitely a passion, but I'm here trying to help Gil." Once I finish telling him my plans, Bash punches me hard in the arm. I grab my biceps and scowl. "What the hell was that for?"

"For you trying to do this on your own when you have a whole goddamn team of SEALs ready and willing to back you up."

I rake my fingers through my damp hair. "This is supposed to be under the radar. I need to work low key on this, Bash."

"Fine, work your angles, but you're doing it as a shadow member of BLACK Security, where you'll have the resources to make your job efficient and safe. When is this next fight happening?"

I shrug. "It has to be rescheduled."

Hooking his arm around his bent knee, Bash says, "Talia asked me to check on Cass. To make sure she's doing okay."

My brows pull together as realization dawns. "*That's* how you found me."

Sebastian grins. "Yeah, so I had a little help, but could you have Cass call Talia."

"I see Talia's got you whipped already." This time I punch him in the arm. "That's for getting married without me as your best man."

He frowns and rubs his muscle. "Stop being an ass and

disappearing on your family and maybe next time you'll be included. But seriously, Talia's concerned about Cass. She thought Cass would touch base last night but she didn't. And now she's not answering her apartment phone or replying to texts or calls to her cell."

My chest tightens. "I don't think she went home. She left in the middle of the night. I don't know the full story as to why she's staying at the Carver estate, but I know she planned to go back."

Sebastian pulls out his phone and sends Talia a text telling her that Cass is at the Carvers.

He starts to say something when his phone rings. "Hey Talia...what's wrong?"

Cutting his gaze to me, he says, "Talia's officially worried for Cass. Mina just told her that rumors are flying around about the police being at the Carver's home late last night. Something about Celeste's ID and some blood found in an abandoned car."

With my heart jerking, I jump up and head for the door, calling over my shoulder, "Make my shadow role at BLACK Security official. I might need that access to your team a lot sooner."

"Done, but Cald..." Bash grabs my arm and pulls me to a stop. "Once this is EUC group is taken down, I want you on my BLACK Security team as my full partner."

His insistence makes me feel divided between loyalty to a true brother and the loner status I've existed in for a while now. I hold his gaze, knowing there's stuff I haven't told him. "We'll discuss it later," I say with a grunt.

Sebastian doesn't like my answer, but nods his agreement and releases me. "I'll use my police resources to find out what they know about the blood they found. What are you planning to do?"

"Find Cass and keep her safe."

CHAPTER TWENTY-FOUR

THE OBSERVER

I wash her blood off my hands in the sink. Red rivets turning pink as they circle the drain. Blood of life. She's mine now forever and ever. It had to be this way; I have no regrets. Now no one can touch her.

* * *

Thank you for reading **GOLD SHIMMER! Find out what happens next! STEEL RUSH (IN THE SHADOWS, Book 5) is NOW AVAILABLE!**

STEEL RUSH

P. T. MICHELLE

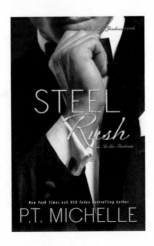

Cass has spent years trying to forget her past. But the thing about pasts...they always come back around, sometimes in the most unexpected ways. When Celeste goes missing, Cass discovers how intricately entangled her past and present are with Celeste's, making it impossible to walk away.

In an effort to ignore his own painful history, Calder challenges a corrupt, underground organization, but his mission gets sidelined when Cass's life becomes endangered.

The passion simmering between Calder and Cass tempts them to share their darkest secrets, but can their trust in each other help them unravel the mystery surrounding Celeste? Can they eliminate the threat to Cass before the past overshadows the present and destroys their intense connection?

Ready to find out what happened?
STEEL RUSH is now available!

See below for a brief excerpt from STEEL RUSH

Calder

Hearing Cass laugh at whatever Ben's saying grates, but the fact she doesn't appear to have her guard up at all is unacceptable. She should've put layers between them. Real, physical layers. Like gloves. Where are the fucking gloves I insisted she put in her pockets? And why is he blowing his goddamn breath on her hands?

My shoulders tense and I ignore the cold air blowing around me as I work to gain control of my thoughts. I'm the only person Cass should trust enough to get that close to her. Hemming doesn't know that her confident smile hides a deep hurt from her past.

Watching him bend close as he whispers something in her ear, it's hard to reconcile the near impenetrable wall I had to break through to be with her the other night, and even then she didn't tell me everything. It might be irrational, but I don't give a damn that she's pretending to be someone else. She needs to employ that wall of distrust with *him*. She needs to be wary.

When Ben lifts her hand and her broad smile fades slightly, I'm instantly on alert. My gut twists as he slides a ring on her left finger. What kind of business-only marriage needs a diamond big enough for me to see from this distance? But it's the look in his eyes as he presses a lingering kiss to the ring on her finger that ignites fierce territorial instincts within me. *Fuck, he wants her.*

One-Click STEEL RUSH now!

If you found **GOLD SHIMMER** an entertaining and enjoyable read, while you're on the retailer picking up **STEEL RUSH**, I hope you'll consider taking the time to leave a review for **GOLD SHIMMER** and share your thoughts in the online bookstore . Your review could be the one to help another reader decide to read GOLD SHIMMER and the other books in the IN THE SHADOWS series!

To keep up-to-date when the next P.T. Michelle book will release, join my free newsletter http://bit.ly/11tqAQN . An email will come straight to your inbox on the day a new book releases.

IF YOU'VE ALREADY READ MISTER BLACK, SCAR-LETT RED and BLACKEST RED and learned about how Sebastian and Talia met, did you know there are more Sebastian and Talia books? Want to read about Sebastian and Talia's wedding in front of friends and family? What about the birth of their child? Then be sure the check out the **IN THE SHADOWS** series list below. *I do write my novels in chronological order, so reading the books in the series in the order they've been written in will give you the richest reading experience by*

keeping the events in all the characters' relationships in order. Here's the reading order below...

Mister Black (Book 1 - Talia & Sebastian, Part 1)
Scarlett Red (Book 2 - Talia & Sebastian, Part 2)
Blackest Red (Book 3 - Talia & Sebastian, Part 3)
Gold Shimmer (Book 4 - Cass & Calder, Part 1)
Steel Rush (Book 5 - Cass & Calder, Part 2)
Black Platinum (Book 6 - Talia & Sebastian, Stand Alone Novel)
Reddest Black (Book 7 - Talia & Sebastian, Stand Alone Novel)
Blood Rose (Book 8 - Cass & Calder, Stand Alone Novel)
Noble Brit (Book 9 - Mina & Den, Stand Alone Novel - Coming March 2019)

Did you know there are **audiobooks** for the **IN THE SHADOWS** series? The audiobooks bring these stories to a whole new level. You can listen to samples and check them out on Audible and iTunes.

IF YOU'RE interested in other contemporary romances by me, check out my **BAD IN BOOTS** series written under Patrice Michelle.

IF YOU'D LIKE to read another epic romance story like the

IN THE SHADOWS books—the kind of love story that spans across several books—check out my **BRIGHTEST KIND OF DARKNESS** series written under P.T. Michelle. These books were written to be enjoyed equally by upper teens 16+ and adults.

Desire (Book 4)
Awaken (Book 5)

Other works by P.T. Michelle writing as Patrice Michelle

Bad in Boots series
(Contemporary Romance, 18+)
Harm's Hunger
Ty's Temptation
Colt's Choice
Josh's Justice

Kendrian Vampires series
(Paranormal Romance, 18+)
A Taste for Passion
A Taste for Revenge
A Taste for Control

Stay up-to-date on her latest releases:

Join P.T's Newsletter:
http://bit.ly/11tqAQN

Visit P.T. :
Website: http://www.ptmichelle.com
Twitter: https://twitter.com/PT_Michelle

Facebook:
https://www.facebook.com/PTMichelleAuthor
Instagram: http://instagram.com/p.t.michelle
Goodreads:
http://www.goodreads.com/author/show/4862274.P_T_M
ichelle

P.T. Michelle's Facebook Readers' Group:
https://www.facebook.com/groups/PTMichelleReadersGr
oup/

ACKNOWLEDGEMENTS

To my fabulous beta readers: Joey Berube, Amy Bensette, and Magen Chambers, thank you for reading *Gold Shimmer* so quickly and for being tough on me so that this book shines. You ladies definitely helped make *Gold Shimmer* a fantastic reading experience.

To my wonderful critique partner, Trisha Wolfe, thank you for reading *Gold Shimmer* more than once! And also for your fabulous critiques, brainstorming sessions, and cheerleading skills. Major hugs, girl!

To my family, thank you for understanding the time and effort each book takes. I love you all and truly appreciate your unending support.

To my amazing fans, thank you for loving my books and for truly broadening my audience with your mad love of the IN THE SHADOWS series and characters! I appreciate each and every one of you for spreading the word by posting reviews and telling all your reader friends about the series whenever you get a chance. Thank you for all the fantastic support you continually give!

ABOUT THE AUTHOR

P.T. Michelle is the *NEW YORK TIMES, USA TODAY*, and International bestselling author of the contemporary romance series IN THE SHADOWS, the YA/New Adult crossover series BRIGHTEST KIND OF DARKNESS, and the romance series: BAD IN BOOTS, KENDRIAN VAMPIRES and SCIONS (listed under Patrice Michelle). She keeps a spiral notepad with her at all times, even on her nightstand. When P.T. isn't writing, she can usually be found reading or taking pictures of landscapes, sunsets and anything beautiful or odd in nature.

To keep up-to-date when the next P.T. Michelle book will release, join P.T.'s free newsletter.

www.ptmichelle.com

Made in United States
North Haven, CT
27 August 2023

40783510R00174